PRINCE OF WALES FORT,
1770

Prince of Wales Fort, 1770

by Katie Churchill-King

© Copyright 2024 Katie Churchill-King

ISBN 979-8-88824-670-2

All rights reserved. No part of this publication may be reproduced, stored in a retrieval system, or transmitted in any form or by any means—electronic, mechanical, photocopy, recording, or any other—except for brief quotations in printed reviews, without the prior written permission of the author.

This is a work of fiction. All the characters in this book are fictitious, and any resemblance to actual persons, living or dead, is purely coincidental. The names, incidents, dialogue, and opinions expressed are products of the author's imagination and are not to be construed as real.

Cover design by Lauren Sheldon

Cover Art:
Hudson's Bay Company Archives, Archives of Manitoba, "A North West View of Prince of Wales's Fort in Hudsons Bay, North America," by Samuel Hearne, 1777. Engraving, black & white. J. Saunders (Engraver). Plate 1, facing page 1, taken from A journey from Prince of Wales's Fort, in Hudson's Bay, to the northern ocean : undertaken by order of the Hudson's Bay Company for the discovery of copper mines, a north west passage, & c. in the years 1769, 1770, 1771 & 1772, by Samuel Hearne

Map credits:
Hudson's Bay Company Archives, Archives of Manitoba, Hudson's Bay Company manuscript maps collection, "A Plan of Part of Hudson's-Bay & Rivers communicating With the Principal Settlements," [1772?], G.2/15, Cartographer: Andrew Graham. Public Domain. Hudson's Bay Company Archives, Archives of Manitoba are holders of the original.

Hudson's Bay Company Archives, Archives of Manitoba, Hudson's Bay Company manuscript maps collection, "A Map of part of the Inland Country to the Nh Wt of Prince of Wale's Fort HB; By, Humbly Inscribed to the Govnr. Depy. Govnr. and Committee of the Honble. Hudns. By. Compy. By their Honrs. moste obedient humble servant Saml. Hearne; 1772." G.2/10. Public Domain. Hudson's Bay Company Archives, Archives of Manitoba are holders of the original.

Published by

◀köehlerbooks™

3705 Shore Drive
Virginia Beach, VA 23455
800-435-4811
www.koehlerbooks.com

PRINCE OF WALES FORT, 1770

KATIE CHURCHILL-KING

VIRGINIA BEACH
CAPE CHARLES

Special thanks to my children Elise, Joe, and Ozzie.
My husband Richard. And Professor Adams as well as my fellow writers of ENG 507 Fall 2023.

This novella takes place between August and December in the year 1770 at Prince of Wales Fort, the ruins of which can still be seen on a point visible from Churchill, Manitoba, Canada. The following characters within the novella are loosely based on historical figures: Keelshies, Moses Norton, Mary Norton, Samuel Hearne, and Matonabbee. These individuals resided at or visited the Fort during the interval of time covered in the novella. The Author's Note at the conclusion of the novella provides reference and source material for interested readers.

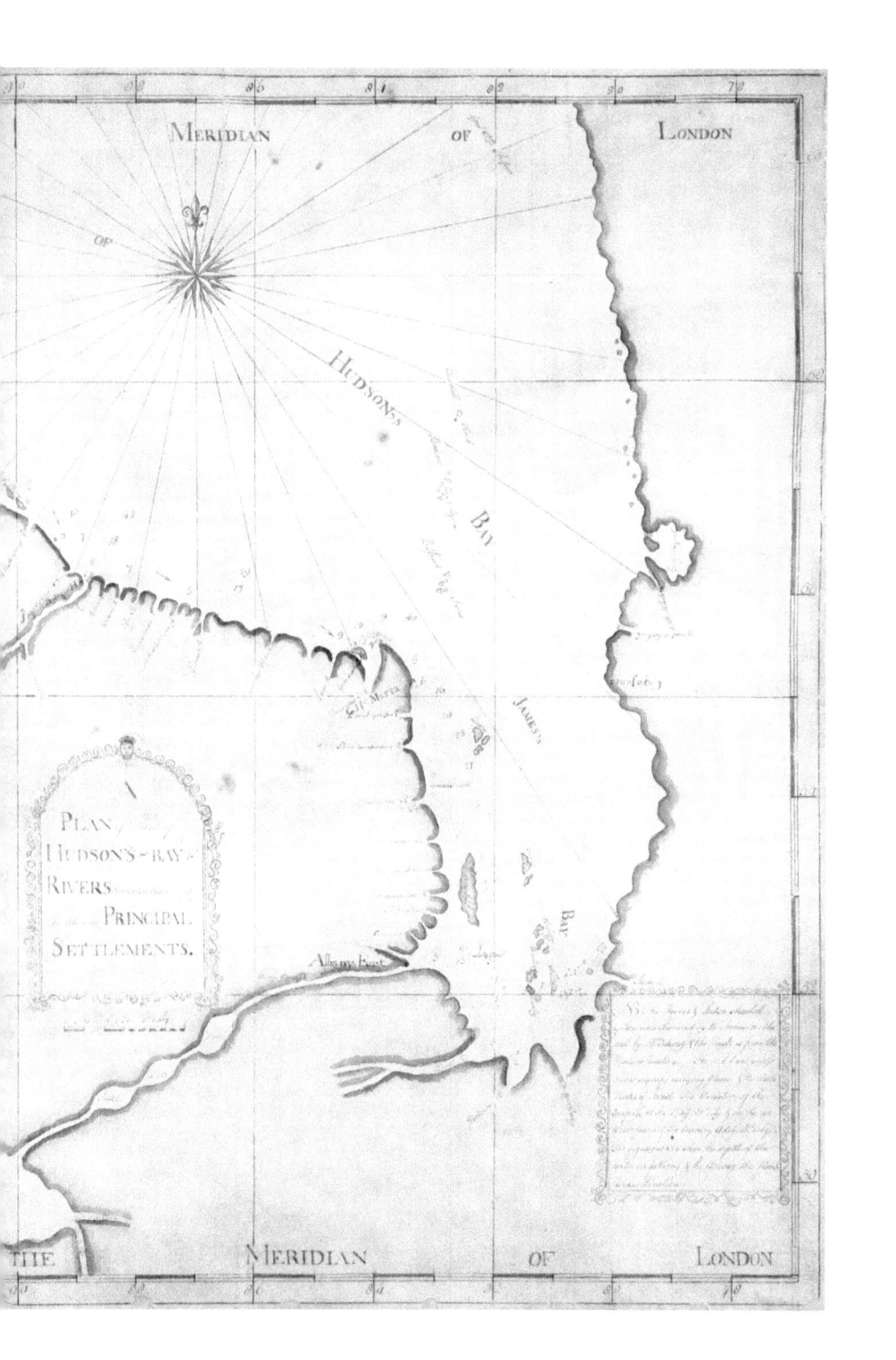

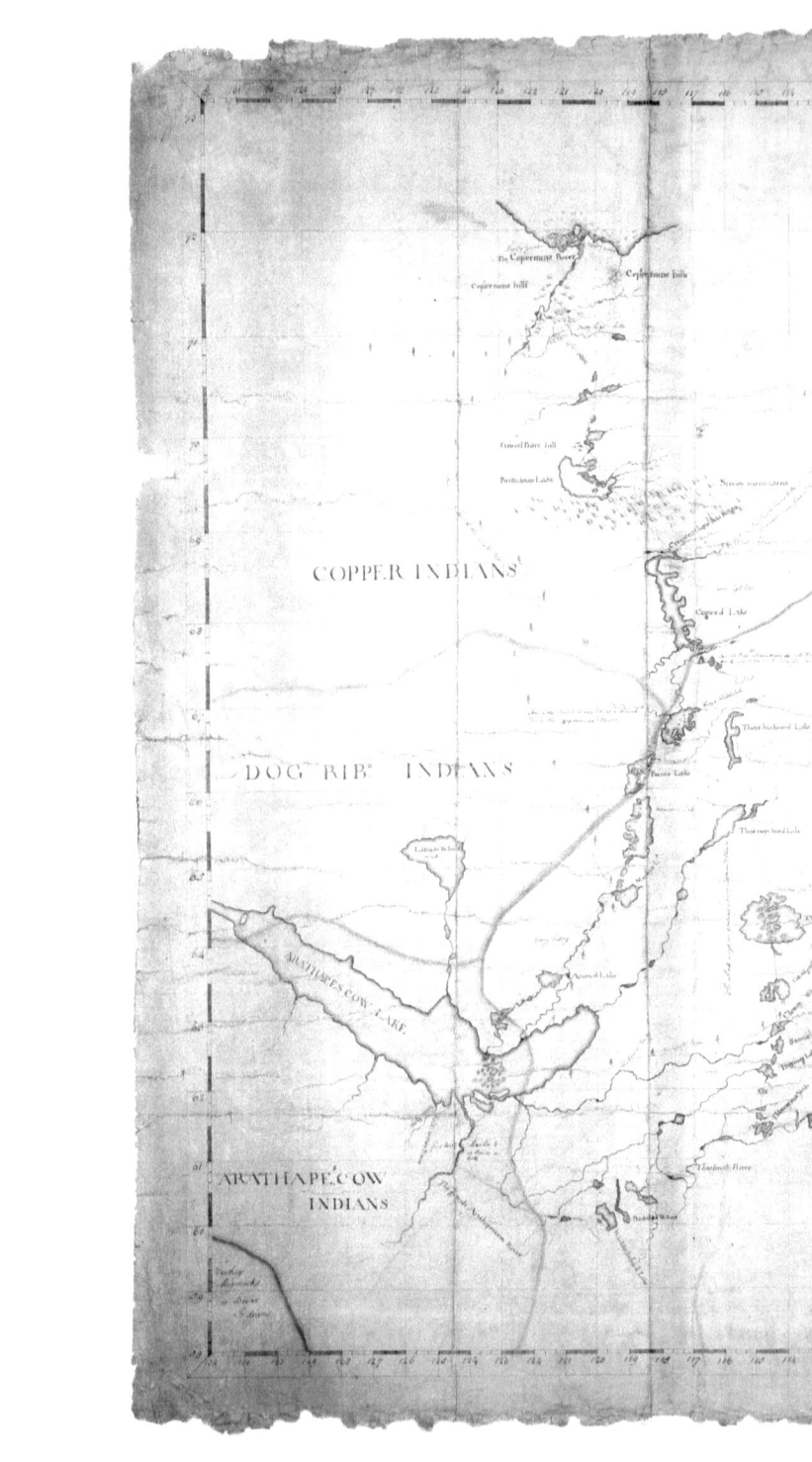

I

Shenandoah steered the canoe, while the favored wife of Chief Keelshies sat high in the middle on a bundle of cooking and tent supplies. Shenandoah, also called Shenan, sat on tent poles, the ends poking her from all sides. Keelshies's wife looked very fine in a soft caribou smock embroidered with a weaving motif of green and blue flowers. The young woman's hair lay in thick braids down her back, stripes of red and black on each cheek. Shenan had watched as, for hours, the woman's sisters had massaged fat down her arms, legs, and hair. Her skin shone and glistened in the sun. Shenan's copper amulet, now around this woman's neck, had been polished with fine sand to a brilliant reddish-gold.

Shenan "the slave," as these people continued to call her, and Waawaatee, "the old woman," by contrast, had barely survived the winter. Waawaatee manned the bow, her paddling staid and steady, with no strength an Elder should possess whose cooking pot was perpetually empty. Shenan knew they were meant to starve, though Chief Keelshies had underestimated Waawaatee and Shenan. The pair was gaunt, their shirt and trousers a patchwork of caribou, muskrat, and rabbit skins. Their hair was clean and tended, though they had no comb, and their nails scrubbed vigorously with brown moss. Shenan, for her part, had the steely gaze of a half-starved girl who would cut any thief in the night that tried to steal her few possessions.

She steered down Churchill River, trailing behind a procession of thirty canoes, the first twenty paddled by men and piled high with furs. Chief Keelshies and his brother led the formation, a flag of red stripes on a white and blue background flying in their stern. Shenan noted that the Chipewyans did not understand the significance of this fabric, beyond the fact that it had been a gift and was important to their trading partners. Shenan, raised near the English, knew it to be the Union Jack. A few other canoes had sticks with colored bits of cloth whipping in the breeze.

The river widened, and the smell of the ocean, before faint, now permeated the air. The waves rocked the canoes, and Chief Keelshies guided toward shore. He held up his hand, and the brigade stopped, the water sloshing against the sides. Keelshies's beautiful wife gripped the canoe, and the party tottered like toys. The outline of Prince of Wales Fort was just discernable, dark stone walls that stretched across the point. Keelshies and some other men fired shots in the air, and they waited.

After perhaps five minutes, or perhaps long enough for the Englishmen to finish their noonday meal, a glass of port, and say some prayers. Shenandoah could only say it was an eternity, in a canoe bobbing violently and taking on water. From the Fort came the firing of guns and discharge of cannon, an explosion of noise and greeting. The Chipewyan men whooped as paddles dipped brisk and purposeful. Keelshies's wife gave Shenan a pointed look, which she understood to mean *We will be the first canoe of women.* And they were; Shenan, with head bowed and graceful dips of her paddle, wove her way and edged into position.

II

Jeremiah had been lectured about this moment since he arrived in Hudson's Bay two weeks before on that wretched ship.

"You will hear the cannon, boy, and first be sure it isn't the damned French. Do you set to task or grab a gun?"

"Grab your gun anyway, son, the Natives could be sent by the French."

"Nonsense, boy, Natives with canoes full of furs are here to trade. Anyone with sense knows that."

In this way, the conversation went in the mess hall after evening meals. The bored Englishmen, drinking their bitter spruce beer, imparting advice to the men fresh off the boat and to Jeremiah "boy," "son," or "Hospital Kid."

"Christ's Hospital, school for boys," grumbled one laborer. "If those rich men in London had schools that cost nothing when I was a boy . . ." The man pointed a rough and dirty finger at Jeremiah, then said, "You best think on that, Hospital Boy, learning to read and write, figures, making charts and the like."

The cannon had fired, and Jeremiah trusted that the sentries were keen on the difference between a Native trading party and a French war party. No shouts of alarm ran through the Fort, only men hurrying to their posts. "Heave!" he heard a man cry as the Englishmen hoisted the Great Flag. Jeremiah rushed to his room and dressed in the regimental coat of black broadcloth with gold piping and epaulettes, given to him just last evening after a discussion in the officers' dining room.

"Governor Norton," the portly Sir George Spurrell had boomed at the dinner, "we must give thought to the man who will be standard bearer when the next trading party arrives. What a disgrace, the drunken laborer from the Orkneys, tipping and nearly hitting one of the Natives with his pole!"

Governor Norton, whose beady black eyes and cold stare made icy fingers creep up Jeremiah's throat, had looked at Sir George in his unfathomable way, making no answer, until all the officers shifted uncomfortably in their seats.

Jeremiah had meekly raised his hand. "Well, gentlemen, I could do it." He only saw men of distinction carry standards in London, though if the laborers from the Orkney Islands were being asked, he supposed he would do.

Jeremiah knew himself to be a child, a boy, now almost a man, a person who could never tolerate an awkward silence and was always the one to raise his hand. In this way, he found himself in yet another perplexing situation, wearing a coat too short for his rail tall frame, a three-pointed hat, and carrying a flagpole. He found his place in the procession, behind the officers and next to the drummers and buglers. They began a proud and windy march to shore, where the beat of the drums and notes of the bugles washed out to sea.

When the cannon went off, goods were pushed hastily against the walls of the trading room and a space cleared in the center. The Chipewyan men followed the merry procession that greeted them and now sat on chairs arranged in a circle. Governor Norton presided in an armchair, Chief Keelshies at his side, and before them stood a table laid with a new beaver coat. On the coat sat a collection of calumets—pipes, of assorted lengths and colors, decorated with engravings, feathers, and beads. The calumet of Chief Keelshies rose above the rest, crested with the brilliant red of a woodpecker forehead.

Each pipe was selected in turn by Chief Keelshies then handed to the governor, who filled it with Brazil tobacco. After lighting, the governor presented the stem to the horizon where the sun rose, to the sky where the sun lives at midday, and to the horizon where the sun sets. A shout went up in the room, and the pipe was passed until spent.

After all the pipes were smoked, the speeches commenced. An Elder began, his voice commanding and somber, musical with its rise and fall. Jeremiah found the sway and rhythm of his words soothing, though he knew none of the language. When the old man stopped, an expectant silence hovered in the room.

All were waiting for the translator, Jeremiah realized. Daniel Bricker was the man who knew the Chipewyan language and Jeremiah craned his neck to locate him.

"Daniel Bricker has taken ill," announced the surgeon, who was standing by the door that led to the Fort's interior. Jeremiah realized that the surgeon was the only officer not present for the march to shore. "And, I regret, sir, I am not aware of another employee with command of the language." The surgeon pantomimed to Chief Keelshies, hand gesturing from his mouth like someone speaking, vigorous shakes of his head, no. He looked ridiculous, but the Natives appeared to understand.

The Chipewyans began to conference, a long and quiet discussion that lasted until the tobacco smell had drifted out of the room, and the men sat again amongst the odors of the sea, mildewed cloth, and musty barrels. Keelshies then inclined his head toward one of the young men, who rose and left.

The chief made a motion with his hands, slowly descending his palms toward the floor. Jeremiah could only think this meant steady, or wait. Governor Norton nodded, as though he understood the gesture.

The governor then motioned to the warehouse keeper, who signaled to his assistants, one of whom was Jeremiah. The governor was using this opportunity to make the gift of clothes, Jeremiah realized. He and another man leapt to action and went to the hall outside the trading room, where hung a complete outfit and an outrageous hat.

Jeremiah inclined his head and handed the hat, a peculiar object, to Chief Keelshies. A wool sash was tied round the crown, and tucked in the sash was a silk handkerchief and feathers of various bright colors. Keelshies respectfully admired the hat and set of clothes then passed them to the other Natives, who ran their fingers along the lace of the coat and curiously stroked the dyed feathers.

The Chipewyan returned. Someone stood behind the young man, obscured from view. Keelshies said a few words, and a young girl was nudged forward. She was perhaps twelve or thirteen years old, hollow-cheeked and obviously underfed. She wore a fine, enormous beaver robe, which did not hide her bony frame, threadbare patched trousers, and lack of shoes.

She lifted her head and her eyes were burning, Jeremiah could not tell in defiance or from hunger. She took up position behind Keelshies.

The Elder began to speak again, and when he stopped, the girl translated in nearly perfect English. "We leave the calumet with our friends, the English. We do not go to the French. Here a great many young men come. Use them kindly! Last year, the powder was measured short and poor quality. Tell your servants to fill the measure and not to put their fingers within the brim; tell your chiefs across the water to send powder like fine sand, not rough dirt."

Though the girl was speaking, her presence became unimportant; she looked only at the Elder, and when his voice rose with emotion or lowered, her voice did as well. She became an extension of the old man and effectually disappeared in the room, like the furniture or walls.

"Give us good Brazil black tobacco moist and hard twisted. Let us see it before opened. The guns are heavy. Give us light and small in hand, and well-shaped, with locks that will not freeze in winter. The young men, they like the red gun cases, and give the roll tobacco cheap. For the women, kettles thick high for the shape and size, strong ears. Do not cut the cloth short."

Jeremiah could now understand the speech thanks to the girl. He studied her and wondered at her skill. Where had she come from—New France perhaps? It was now part of the British Empire but still mostly French. She did not appear important within this tribe, vagabond as she was. He tried to recall maps of America, maps where rivers and terrain, charted and explored, faded into white, where no European had gone before. She was a long way, an improbable distance, from any English settlement.

The Elder, and the girl in turn, raised their fists and cried, "Give us good measure! Give us good measure!"

III

Jeremiah had been uninvited from the officers' dinner; Chief Keelshies and his lieutenants would be attending, and his seat was taken. After enduring barking orders from the warehouse keeper, reassembling the trading room, and doing inventory yet again on the brandy, beads, and vermilion, Jeremiah had finally been able to retire to his room.

His head was swimming, and he tried to conjure happy memories of home. His conversation with the warehouse keeper now disturbed his thoughts.

Jeremiah had balked at the prospect of doing the inventory for a third time today on those items and said as much to the keeper, who replied, "That's one means of making our overplus, son."

Jeremiah was confused, and the keeper let out an exasperated sigh and said, "Anything, boy, measured in yard, pound, or gallon. There's no cutting an inch off a gun or taking a few ounces off an awl, though we find ways to trade those up as well."

As he lay in his bed, Jeremiah better understood the Elder's speech, calling for fair and honest treatment. The company employees did intend to cut the cloth short and measure the beads light. The behavior of these Englishmen was at odds with the rules and training he received from the Hudson's Bay Company in London.

A knock came at the doorframe, and through the soiled and

tattered curtain that substituted for a solid door peered the little face of John America Norton, the son of Governor Norton.

"Come in, John," and Jeremiah motioned for the boy to enter. John America had been Jeremiah's savior when he arrived at the Bay three weeks ago, dreadfully sick from that hellish ship. John America brought him fish broth for three days and the two had become fast friends, though Jeremiah had not seen the boy for a few days. "Where have you been off to?"

"Oh, with my mother, sir." John's mother lived, best Jeremiah could tell, half a day's journey from the Fort, where the forest began. She lived there with her Cree family, unless, as John put it, "summoned by Father."

"Mother and I saw the trading party, and she sent me with roots, greens, and the like for the officers' salad."

"Ahh, yes I see," said Jeremiah, although he didn't really, as the farthest he had stepped from the Fort was to carry the standard to the water's edge.

"I've come for you, sir, as the cooper prepared your dinner and I fear he has not done it squarely."

Jeremiah was hungry, of course. He was always hungry. He had been stuck in the warehouse, doing inventory, and suspected as much that the cooper would be again pilfering from his rations. When he arrived, he learned that he would be pooled with three other men, and they would prepare their meals together each evening. Referred to as a "mess" in the navy, Jeremiah had counted his blessings that his mess contained the cooper, who was a tolerable cook. That was until he realized that the cooper enjoyed his own ration of one-pound meat and an extra half pound to boot, as long as that extra half pound belonged to Jeremiah.

"Thank you for telling me, young sir," said Jeremiah, rising and patting the little fellow on the head as he went to see what remained of his supper.

The conversation was animated in the mess hall that evening. The arrival of the Natives, their dress, manners, and events of the day enlivened the room; even the dark stone walls seemed brighter. Jeremiah was in luck as his plate sat, although missing his biscuit, intact. Unfortunately, it was placed next to Rodney Smith, a crass though knowledgeable company employee.

As Jeremiah ate, Rodney expounded upon one of his favorite topics. Each man needed their "bit of brown" or a Cree woman, with which to pass the winter.

"The company doesn't want you loafing, mulling about the Fort all winter, eating from the stock room till it's bare. Best to winter away, son, trap some furs, or better yet have your woman do it. Company pays you half what they fetch in London."

More than one employee had counseled Jeremiah to winter away with his "country wife." He was told the woman was essential, as she could hunt, trap, fish, collect firewood, sew, and cook. Without the woman, they all said, a man would freeze and starve. Since first given this advice, Jeremiah had the same burning question.

"What happens if," Jeremiah said, turning red, "she ends up with child?"

Rodney whooped and slapped Jeremiah on the back. "They aren't Christian, boy. Once your contract is over and you return to England, you never give them another thought."

Jeremiah was taken aback. "Well, that doesn't seem right. What becomes of the child?"

"Oh, well, you could give her father a little tobacco, give her some beads, maybe the littles a bit of oatmeal." Rodney could see Jeremiah was not content with this answer. "Some of the finer gentlemen, they pension them off, you know. Can you imagine? Every year, they set aside a bit of their pension to give these brats. And there's even talk of a school! On the Orkneys. I have a wife and four children in England, myself." Rodney leaned in close, and Jeremiah wasn't sure if he smelled the man's teeth or clothes. "I certain have a few out there." He chuckled, almost merrily, and motioned in the direction of the forest where John America had come from.

Their conversation was interrupted by yelling and the harsh scrape of benches. A mug hit the wall above Jeremiah's head, the beer pouring in his hair and drenching his shirt. When hired, the London Committee were firm that fighting was forbidden and would result in loss of wages for the entire season. However, he could tell from his two-week residence that the Orkney men fought almost nightly, and this was to be a particularly nasty skirmish. The spruce beer he wore was portioned, and the man who lost it would get no more.

Jeremiah slunk away with his back to the wall and fingers gripping the stone groove, inching himself toward the door.

A voice cut through the cacophony, sharp and biting like a chisel: "Enough!" The men froze in place, and Jeremiah saw the governor standing at the door, his black eyes burning like smoldering coals. "Out," he said, his tone low and dangerous. The men all filed toward the door, sullen and feet dragging. As Jeremiah exited, his eyes shifted to avoid the governor's gaze, but the man spoke to him.

"You are needed to serve the officers' dinner. Change your clothes."

IV

The fine caribou shirt that Shenandoah wore felt soft, and her fingers itched to touch the intricate beaded pattern at the collar. Chief Keelshies's eldest wife had handed Shenan the valuable outfit with clear instructions: After the officers' dinner, she would return directly to this woman's tent, give back the clothing, and change into her old rags. For two years, Shenan had not worn anything that was not patched, puckered, or full of holes. She curled her toes in the soft moccasins, luxurious and so unlike her last pair of shoes, a sad medley of blanket scraps, flannel, and molded bits of hide.

Uncle Andrew was a drunken sot who deserved to drown in his own vomit or be murdered by his endless line of unsavory friends and associates. He never would, the golden boy and carrier of the family legacy. *No one is even looking for me,* Shenan thought. *I am a Montour. I'm Shenandoah Montour, and no one even cares.*

Her life had changed completely two years ago when Uncle Andrew abandoned her. She could still see the steely grey sky and smell the sooty acrid fire. She had opened her eyes to see the two French voyageurs watching her. They had awakened, alert as cats, though stinking drunk the night before. She knew then that the bastard, Uncle Andrew, had left her because no one remained to say her name. That fateful morning marked three years since Meme had died.

A loud voice pierced her reverie. "Could one of you gentleman wake the squaw? She is here to translate, is she not?"

Shenan focused on the voice, a red-faced rotund man she heard others call Sir George.

"Ahh, ask them, girl, about the copper that his woman wore." Sir George pointed at Chief Keelshies, who bristled at the fat finger.

"Sir George," admonished the surgeon and looked at her kindly. "The situation, my child, is that we have a man by the name of Samuel Hearne on an expedition to the North with a Native guide in search of a copper mine and other precious metals. For this reason, we are interested in how Chief Keelshies came about this copper jewelry that we saw his wife wearing."

Shenan translated, knowing the copper amulet belonged to her and had nothing to do with Keelshies or some Northern mine. She remembered this man, Hearne. Their parties had crossed paths when traveling to the Fort going in opposite directions, and she never knew the aim of his expedition. At the time, she was still barely surviving and only able to secure a little food every three days while hauling over sixty pounds on her back.

She hadn't given him much thought, as the Englishman had no dedicated servant and hung at the fringes of camp. She had seen this type. He was a source of shot and powder, an amusement, a man to fill a pipe. To her, he was a like a bird that caught the wrong wind, a curiosity perched on a limb, that might be killed by a passerby for the feathers to decorate his bag.

Keelshies responded, "The governor should have sent a man last spring and told me he was looking for a guide. The guide you chose is my acquaintance and winters at Seal River. He knows nothing of the far Northern lands."

Governor Norton said, "The man arrived at the Fort after Hearne's first failed attempt and offered himself as chief guide. If this expedition is not successful, we can discuss Chief Keelshies leading out the next."

After Shenan spoke, Keelshies said, "Such a journey would involve travel through many seasons and lands belonging to numerous families and chiefs. We would need substantial gifts to safely pass."

"Of course," said the governor, following Shenan's translation. "The company would provide ample resources for your people, if another such journey were approved by our directors across the Great Sea."

After Shenan spoke, Keelshies seemed pleased, and reclined his head in assent.

"Have we determined, gentlemen, whether the copper used for the jewelry is from the mine for which Mr. Hearne has been searching these last eighteen months?" boomed Sir George, and Shenan obliged.

Chief Keelshies said, "We know of this copper source. We have seen the copper. We own kettles, arrowheads, and ice chisels made from copper. My people do not wear jewelry made from this metal." The chief scoffed. Shenan readily translated, knowing that he was making a mistake. Keelshies should claim ownership of the jewelry, which would be easy enough, his own wife wearing it.

Keelshies disdained copper jewelry. Shenan could not determine the reason, except that his enemies, the Esquimaux, wore this metal as an adornment. Other Chipewyan groups they came across wore jewelry fashioned from it. His people owned utilitarian items made of copper, but Keelshies objected to its use as jewelry. His wife happened to be enamored of Shenan's amulet; indeed, the young woman had insisted upon its purchase when Shenan was handed over by the voyageurs. Keelshies had appeared ambivalent when they launched the canoes and he saw her wearing it. He did not understand that the English neither knew nor understood his disdain for copper jewelry, as related to his enemies or whatever his reason could be. He would grow in their esteem if he claimed the amulet, connecting him with the copper mine that these Englishmen appeared to be seeking. Shenan understood all of this because she understood the English, having dealt with them all her life.

"The jewelry belongs to the slave." Keelshies waved dismissively at Shenan, and she gleefully translated.

The Englishmen all turned to look at her.

"How child," asked the surgeon, "did you come by this jewelry?"

I am a vagabond child to them, Shenan thought, *cared for by no one and unimportant. And indeed I am, but they will not know it.* Meme had taught her many important lessons in the short time that she was old enough to know her. One of them: It does not matter who you are but who you say you are.

Shenandoah began her narrative. She told them she was the niece of Andrew Montour and granddaughter of Madame Isabelle Montour, translators famed from Hudson River Valley to Michilimackinac. Through unfortunate circumstances, and the villainy of two unscrupulous French voyageurs, she had become a slave to these people. Her family was surely distraught and looking for her.

No one, of course, was looking for her. But her speech had the desired effect. The officers' faces showed interest and a little pity. In the corner, a young man dressed in a footman's uniform that was much too short, holding a serving towel and silver tray, cried out, "Gentlemen, we must help this girl!"

Shenan's first winter amongst Keelshies's people had been cold but not hungry. The winter grounds provided; caribou were caught in the hedge traps as they plodded through the snow, and there were the occasional beaver, moose, and small game.

The overplus of caribou, at times in such plenty that they were killed just for the tongues, kept Shenan and Waawaatee in good health. They had a moose hide tent, which kept out the cold and snow, and Waawaatee sewed them moccasins. The old woman with her skill at embroidery and beading even secured them a comb, an axe, and an iron cooking pot.

Keelshies did not travel to Prince of Wales Fort that spring. He said they did not have enough furs for the trouble, but Shenan thought he was comfortable—a full belly, four wives, nights spent around the fire with family, stories, drumming, and dancing. Shenan would glimpse him briefly through the door of his glowing tent, ensconced on a pile of furs, the rich smell of tobacco wafting from the door.

He had traded furs with another Chipewyan chief, by the name of Matonabbee, in exchange for tobacco, shot, and powder. Also, some guns, blankets, and cooking pots to replace the damaged and run down. He was not in urgent need of goods nor eager for the journey.

The second winter, this past winter, was different. The usual winter grounds did not provide. Waawaatee told Shenan that there were winters when the game did not come and there appeared to be resignation, acceptance, on the part of the Chipewyans. One day, when the hedge traps were empty yet again and the dried meat was nearly gone, they left their forest enclave and went in search across the barren plains.

The occasional caribou was killed and eaten first by Keelshies, then his men, then the boys, then the wives, with nothing left for the girls, elderly, or "slave." These unfortunates would eat anything, whatever raw scraps remained in the snow or fell beside the fire. If that failed, they ate their clothes and shoes.

At first, the group moved purposefully, the men branching out, hunting the area, the women pushing ahead to camp. The women would set up, and as dusk fell, hunters were seen on the horizon, walking heavily on snowshoes, heads hanging and empty-handed. No caribou were seen for days on end, then days again, and the band wandered, aimlessly, shells of hunger. The dogs that pulled the sleighs collapsed, their chests rose slowly, one eye staring at the grey sky or looming sun. The sleighs were abandoned or harnessed by a man or woman with no strength left. Not knowing or thinking but doing, no survival without the gun, shot, powder, cooking pot.

The miles of snow, ice, taunting blue sky with full sun and wispy cloud but offering no warmth. Nights in which Shenan dug with a tent pole, then just her hands, a hole in the snow where she and Waawaatee would lie. There were no longer alliances, friendships, politics, intrigues; those who possessed a connection, unexplainable, invisible but there, traveled and stayed together without speaking. They were not two birds in a nest but two souls, circling the lake in a sinking canoe. Then there were those that had no one, and they were like ghosts. They hung at the fringes, stooped under the weight of their packs. In the morning, if they rose, they looked formless, void of color. Without a companion, or their companion gone, they drug their feet with the tread of the dead. Sometimes, the wolves would howl, sensing emptiness, hopelessness. Shenan knew wolves circled impending death, but they also tracked the Spirit.

The survivors eventually found a wooded place, by a lake, that provided cover, firewood, caribou and fish, not aplenty but enough to feed the men. She and Waawaatee made a shelter from boughs and branches, and she warmed her fingers by a fire that the two had managed to start with a few stolen coals. Then, she crept away, the moon high and bright, to set her first trap.

She assembled a noose trap that she witnessed another woman make who was known for her skill. Shenandoah herself had lived the middleman life and knew nothing of making traps. She benefited as a child from the fees and gifts received by Meme and Uncle Andrew in exchange for translations, favors, and connections. Now, hunger made her attune only to activities that involved food. The woman skillful with traps had dug her hole on the barren plains one night next to Shenan. Shenan had watched her with sharp focus. A notch in the large stick, a notch in the small stick, a circle tied from sapling.

"How does it work?" Shenan had asked.

And the woman had fit the notches of the two sticks together, affixed the sapling circle to the smaller stick, and explained that the larger was hammered into the frozen ground. A young tree was relieved of its branches, bent and tied to the smaller stick. The noose must be placed where rabbits would cross, their paths discernable to those with a good eye. Other paths nearby should be piled with brush or other debris or detriment. This way, the rabbit ran right into the noose, and its weight detached the smaller stick from the larger. The bent tree was now set aright, bringing the small stick, sapling, and rabbit up in the air, safe from scavengers.

Shenandoah awoke at the first hint of dawn in this new camp. She remembered her trap, set the night before, and hurried out, checking behind her. No one had stirred. As she neared the trap, she saw only the little tree, still bent and tied. Then she spotted it—a limp rabbit, white as the snow it lay on. She ran, heart in her stomach, and inspected the trap. Sleet in the night had clung to the little tree, so it was frozen in position and had not sprung. She loosened the sapling noose with fingers that seized in the frozen air and felt the soft fur in her hands.

Since the food ran out, Shenan had felt the promise of life was gone. Death would come for her; she was two, maybe three moons from starvation. In the spring, the thaw would uncover her, a pile of rags, bones, a bygone meal of the wolves.

With this rabbit, she saw the promise of life. She could survive these people. Someday, she would tell this tale. She reset the trap.

She took a meandering route back to the pile of brush that served as their tent in hopes that anyone tracking her footsteps would be thrown off and confused, unable to steal her game. The biting air, before adding to her listlessness, invigorated her. She and Waawaatee would sneak away from camp under some pretense, and if not followed, they would skin, cook, and devour this little creature.

Last winter felt unreal and far away as Shenan now stood in a dining room lit by bright candles in wall scones, oak tables placed end to end, and polished mahogany chairs. The chipped china plates were painted with an English countryside scene. The Chipewyans handled the glass goblets with extreme care. Shenan could imagine that the Natives were impressed by the finery despite the smell of close unwashed bodies and black mold in the cracked stone walls. But she also knew that the Chipewyans would be relieved to escape this place and return to the open sky and ocean breeze.

The Chipewyans were standing to leave, and Shenan was translating their words of gratitude. Governor Norton and Chief Keelshies had a brief exchange about tomorrow. The drum would sound, the trading room would open. Respectful bows.

Shenandoah was headed toward the door behind Chief Keelshies, when she heard, "And can you, girl, read and write?"

She turned just enough to see Governor Norton, who was facing the wall with his back to the dining room. He appeared to be making a pretense of adjusting his clothes.

"Yes," she said.

"Can you embroider?"

"Not well, but I was taught."

"Have you ever worked as a lady's maid?"

Was the man in need of a lady's maid? She had been in these northern lands for two years and had not seen even a building nor road never mind an English lady.

"I have not."

Keelshies was moving, and as she followed him, she faintly heard the governor say, "You would do for my daughter, Mary."

Shenan shuffled out behind the line of Chipewyan men. *His daughter, Mary?*

An Englishman escorted the native party by torchlight, with Shenan trailing behind, through the halls of the Fort and to the camp outside the walls. She returned the clothes to Keelshies's eldest wife and collapsed in her own tent on a worn moose fur that Waawaatee had laid out next to quiet red coals. By the time she fixed her eyes on the subtle changes of red and black in the fire, she had many things figured out.

The winds of destiny had blown along her path and were favorable. She was not a lady's maid, but she could become one. Ships must come here from England, with Englishmen and English goods, and perhaps even from Virginia or Massachusetts. In one evening, she was now years ahead of her escape plan that before involved winters of survival and starvation and an unlikely escape. She would walk into Otstonwakin, where she hoped Meme's house still stood, and rain hell on Uncle Andrew.

She thanked the Great Spirit Manitou and the Christian God, both to whom Meme had prayed, and also Nitosi, the Chipewyan God. It did not matter who was responsible, if any of them were.

Just as the rabbit brought her faith when she had lost all hope, this latest turn of events infused her with gratitude. The world was boundless. She was not sure what this Governor Norton intended, but she knew it was a step closer out of this place.

V

Jeremiah was on night watch as punishment, he was certain, because of his outburst at the dinner. The girl's story had shocked his sensibilities, and though his cry to help her was almost involuntary, he was still baffled that his fellow countrymen had not risen to her cause.

Throat clearing, uncomfortable drinks from cups, and napkin rearranging all followed his protestation. From what he remembered, the girl did not translate what he said. Her face was impossible to read.

The surgeon had offered, "Well, we shall see what can be done." And then, "What were your thoughts, Chief Keelshies, on the quality of the guns?"

Now, Jeremiah was shivering, hugging the Fort walls on his rounds, looking through the embrasures and past the cannon. To the north, west, and east, he saw dark waving grass and the sea. From the southwesterly aspect of the Fort, he heard the low hum of voices from the Native's tents and saw their glowing fires.

Jeremiah had given up on a promotion ever in this place. Standard bearer, footman, cackling ass from the corner of the dining room. He was only the butt of the joke, the jester, the fool. Granted, his teachers at Christ's Hospital had suggested he become a lawyer. Mr. Wedderburn had encouraged him toward that career: "Your writing isn't poor, you could talk the hind legs off a donkey, and you have the sensibility of Jesus. Granted, you'll most likely end up penniless and defending the poor in Devil's Acre."

This didn't sound promising or profitable to a young man, especially when his mother and sister were penniless and under the critical eye of an uncharitable aunt. Besides, Jeremiah had read the pamphlets, passed around and devoured by his classmates—swashbuckling pirates, enslaved Englishmen who escaped from savages or were murdered, white sand beaches with coconuts on trees and giant fruit, naked women, cannibals. His classmates at Christ's Hospital hid pamphlets under their mattresses, cracks in the walls, floorboards, anywhere they could whisper to another, "the space behind the hearth, reach to the left."

The boys craved the smells, colors, fights, storms at sea; what young man would want to sit in filthy London, bent over papers all day but Sunday, when he could sail the seas and engage the Spanish pirates and the French? What boy had not read *Robinson Crusoe* a dozen times?

His schoolmates with better connections, superior intelligence, and a hint of swagger were hired by the East India Company. Jeremiah had settled for the Hudson's Bay Company, or they had settled for him. His references were thin and uninspiring, the letters written by his teachers at Christ's Hospital indifferent on his competence, though they recognized his work ethic and enthusiasm. He was most likely considered thanks to Sir William Wales, the famed mathematician and astronomer. Mr. Wales had by no means recommended him to the Hudson's Bay Company, but he trained all the boys at Christ's Hospital in the basics of surveying and mapmaking. Jeremiah did not have a talent for it, but could perhaps, if wandering in the Bay hinterlands, pinpoint his general location. The London Committee had asked him if he would consider undertaking an expedition, if chosen and qualified, after a few years learning the ways of the Bay. When faced with the prospect, death by starving or freezing, perhaps eaten by Natives, his entire being screamed no. Then he thought of Mother and Sister, bent over darning, embroidery, eating like birds, suffering with Aunt. He gave an emphatic, "Yes!" with as much eagerness as he could muster.

He would never be chosen for a journey, which was a step toward promotion, when he was given tasks such as footman and second night watch. And, to top it all, his companion on second watch was Rodney Smith, the same man who liked to brief him on country wives and abandoning his Native children.

Rodney Smith was supposed to take a turn walking the Fort's interior perimeter. However, he was drunk by the gate with two friends and allowing every man who requested exit, though none had permission to leave. Some were laborers, some were officers; it was as though word spread that Rodney was in charge of the small wooden door to the side of the great wooden doors, and they took advantage to visit their women or bring them in.

Jeremiah returned from his round to find that Rodney and his friends had been given chairs to sit on as they passed a brown bottle. The style of the bottle was nothing that the Fort provided from its stores, and Jeremiah assumed it was smuggled on the latest ship. Smuggled by these two friends, Jeremiah thought, as they had been on the same vessel that delivered Jeremiah. Jeremiah didn't know them well; Rodney's two friends had been sullen on the boat, unhappy because they had squandered all their earnings at alehouses in London and had to sign on again with the company. Rodney and these two friends had served together at York Fort, a company fort south of here, Jeremiah recalled.

"Yes, Bricker must have a tender stomach," one of the friends was saying as Jeremiah approached, and the three men snickered. Jeremiah recognized the name of Daniel Bricker, the company man who knew the Chipewyan language.

"My stomach is sensitive as well to arsenic," said the other friend, and Rodney chortled, snorted like a pig and said, "Shh, shh, the boy doesn't know!"

Jeremiah collapsed in the dirt next to the men, exhausted from a full day's work and now a sleepless night. The bottle was passed his way, and his first impulse was to wave it away. But the glass felt good in his hand, and he took a drink, the liquid warming his body.

He could not deny that he was curious about what he didn't know. However, he was in a pensive mood after three turns around this Fort, the stars like bright jewels in the sky and the slow tread of his feet like a drowning drum. He thought about why he was here, not sure. To support his mother and sister, yes, but there was something more. He thought about why Rodney Smith and these two friends were here, most certainly to support their families, but also for this: to sit in the night and drink oneself silly in the cool air, free of the constant hunger and excessive work in England; to have a dalliance with Native women and feel like a king. Common men in England were always reminded, they would always be common.

The stars were like natural streetlights, giving the courtyard a silver hue.

One friend said, "It will be good to have Bricker back, though. Can't have a Native girl translating in the trading room tomorrow. She's most likely a thief."

"What was Bricker's malady?" asked Jeremiah.

"The governor's women," answered the other friend, and the three again shook with poorly contained laughter, falling on each other and merrily taking draughts.

"I'm not understanding," Jeremiah admitted, too tired to feign knowledge of this place. "Are the governor's women sick? How many women does he have?"

Rodney leaned forward and gave Jeremiah a wise look. "It's not how many women he has, son. It's knowing which women are his. Otherwise, you'll end up like Daniel Bricker, or even worse, dead like the blacksmith a few years back."

"How daft, to kill the blacksmith," said one friend, and the three men nodded seriously at this statement.

"Hard to replace," said the other friend, and Jeremiah wasn't sure he'd ever witnessed three comrades more in agreement.

"Now, hold up," said Jeremiah. "Why would the governor poison his only Chipewyan translator when he was expecting them any day?"

"I guess that's what Daniel Bricker thought," said one of the friends, and at this, the men could not contain themselves. Their attempts to shush each other only made the three laugh harder. Between their exasperating drunkenness and ungodly smell now combined with brandy, Jeremiah could take no more. He stood.

"Well, I'm going to do another round," he said.

And they waved him away, arms around each other's shoulders, bodies shaking, hushed whispers at his back.

By the time Jeremiah rounded the corner, Rodney and his friends had reached a different stage in their drunkenness. They were more subdued, their whispers fervent and nervous.

Jeremiah sank down and was again passed the bottle which was much lighter. Every muscle felt tight, and his bones were weary.

"I tell you, I have seen her," one of the friends was whispering, intense and fearful, "only in the governor's house when I bring in the moss and wood, but it's a ghost, I say. Dressed in white, disappears down the corridors and behind doors."

"It's one of his women, you fool," said the other friend.

"No, it's not, you imbecile. His women wear only Native clothes, and," he said, shooting the friend a scathing look, "I make a point to know which ones are his."

A silence ensued. and Jeremiah sensed that the mood was souring. The three men, before compatriots and the best of friends, now looked sulky and glum.

"I'll tell you men a secret," said Rodney, and when he leaned forward, Jeremiah had never seen the man so serious, his eyes direct and mouth a tight line. "I'll even tell the boy. You'll find out soon enough. And best to know, and not go running around, talking about ghosts and making fools of yourselves." Rodney fixed Jeremiah with a pointed look. He had most definitely heard about his outburst at the dinner.

The stars had gone, and it was that sad moment before dawn, when the night is done, the day has yet to begin, and the sky is like a no man's land or most colorless color. Jeremiah and the two friends waited, their faces drawn with fatigue.

"Would you say the governor is English or Native?"

Jeremiah and the friends looked at each other. This was an unexpected question, waiting as they were for a scandalous secret.

"Well, I suppose he's part Native," said one friend, and Jeremiah nodded in agreement. The governor was darker skinned than the average Englishman, but for Jeremiah it was more his way of speaking. He spoke a precise and learned English, correct and near perfect, but the words and pronunciation were careful and measured. His speech struck Jeremiah as that of a man who had come from somewhere else but had studied very hard.

"Well, he is. He's a half-breed, raised here in the Bay, but he tells everyone he's English. He's the son of Richard Norton, a governor from years back, and his Cree wife. But he tells everyone he is the son of Richard Norton and his Englishwoman."

"Well, why would he pretend he's English, and why would anyone believe him?" asked Jeremiah.

Rodney fixed him with an incredulous look. "Could a half-breed be governor?" Rodney shrugged. "And he's a good trader. The company doesn't care, as long as everyone pretends to believe it."

The sky was now lightening, and any moment the morning watch would arrive. Also, the drummers would be coming to play, and the trading room would open, where Jeremiah supposed he would be all day, recording sales.

"Well, that's not even a secret," said one friend, looking peevish and ready for a fight. "I have a cousin in Georgia who pretends he's a baronet. Everyone does that in America."

"No, that wasn't the secret," whispered Rodney. "This fantasma you've seen, this ghost, this white figure in the halls of the governor's house—that's his daughter. He has a daughter that is more Native than him, that he's raised like an English lady, and her name is Mary."

VI

Shenan recognized "The English March" drummed at the first hint of light. She was familiar with this drum beat; she had entered many a Native village with it tapping, trailing behind Meme or Uncle Andrew. This drum song was the English way to signal readiness for ceremony or trade. This morning, it meant the warehouse was open, and the company would now conduct business. The camp was stirring, fires restored with moss. Bread and prunes were the chief breakfast, gifted by the governor to Keelshies. Fresh water, fetched from a nearby stream, was poured into the cooking pots in anticipation of the oatmeal that would soon be purchased.

The women began emerging from their tents, small bundles of furs strapped to their backs. These were the furs that the women themselves had trapped and were permitted to keep for their own purposes. They were not caribou, moose, or musk ox furs, as those required guns. They were not thick and valuable rabbit, marten or fox furs, as those were commandeered by the husbands. The skins and furs in the women's packs were defective, with burn or insect holes in the hide, matted or thin fur. The husbands did not want these furs in their own trade bundles and sent the wives to get what they could.

Waawaatee and Shenandoah, however, had no man to steal their furs. They approached the wooden gangway and were last in line, as planned, with a large bundle. Inside the pack were white rabbit furs, marten furs so glossy and smooth they looked wet, and ermine furs. Shenan was most proud of the ermine, a difficult creature to trap, quick and elusive as it was. She had three, silky and crisp white, with tails that, once released from the tight pack, draped nicely with a black tip. She had heard that the kings of England lined their robes with this ermine fur.

The girl's and old woman's furs almost hadn't made it as the pair had no way to transport them to the Bay without risking confiscation by Keelshies. The two had scraped the hides clean by stealth of night, stretched them far up a tree to dry, worked far from camp so that no one would notice their fires, and massaged a paste of animal brains into the furless side. The resulting hide was soft and pliable.

Shenan had spoken to Waawaatee in hushed whispers in their tent of branches. "Where will we hide them? Do we bury them? Should we pick just a few?" The large bundle of furs would have been conspicuous among their meager possessions; moose hide for a small tent, two ragged blankets, and a few worn cooking items and utensils.

Good fortune arrived as they approached departure, when Keelshies's beautiful wife snapped, "You will carry my bundles, girl." The woman had a large pack of clothing, two heavy blankets, thick moose furs for bedding, combs, beads, more than one looking glass, jewelry, and the list went on. This clever woman had hidden all these goods before the group starved on the barren plains and she and her sisters had gone to fetch them in the spring.

Carrying someone's bundle was a task that required organization; the servant had to locate items quickly. When the woman asked for a comb, she wanted it then. If the woman asked for a child's favorite spoon, Shenan had to know its exact location in the pack. She worried, if she fumbled or delayed, that the impatient woman would shove her aside and start digging, only to discover the furs. By shifting some possessions to Waawaatee and splitting their hard-earned gains, the two had made it, undetected, all the way to Prince of Wales Fort.

Now, as they waited in line, Shenan was hopeful that the goods procured today would sustain Waawaatee through the winter. She sensed that Keelshies, if given the opportunity, would abandon the old woman and leave her to die. The chief was resentful against Waawaatee, for reasons that Shenan never understood.

Keelshies wasn't a chief, really, at least in Shenan's judgment. Unlike the Iroquois, among whom Shenan lived, the Chipewyans had no village where their firekeepers stayed or council met yearly. For the Chipewyans, the fire was wherever they lit it, their council whoever surrounded it.

The corn in Shenan's village didn't walk away, but the caribou of the Chipewyan ambled wherever they pleased. As Waawaatee told it, the caribou may cross the same river, or crop of woods, year after year and then choose a different path, for reasons they didn't share. The Chipewyan would amass on the river shore or weave their hedge traps through the trees, awaiting the arrival of this revered beast, the foundation of their tents, clothes, shoes, sustenance, their lives. And it wouldn't come.

Shenan herself saw the dissolution of community that second hungry winter—family by family breaking away like an ice floe, floating across what appeared to Shenan as vast barren swaths of land.

Keelshies was a skilled hunter and trapper and made gifts to his friends but wasn't called chief until he landed on the shores of Churchill. He, his brothers, and their families had set off, and he gathered people along the way like a rolling, sticky pine cone. Chipewyans would be waiting ahead or be seen across the plains or emerge from the woods and be absorbed into line. A handful of times, new bodies would be sitting by the fire at night, Shenan unsure when they arrived.

The largest contingent was gathered when they built their canoes by the lakeshore. People were waiting, people came, fires were blazing, the fish were plentiful, extended families were reunited, and Shenan worried and fussed over the wife's pack, guarding it like a hungry wolf. Keelshies would make promises. "I am respected at the Fort, I am a friend of the Governor, he gives me many gifts." Some men entrusted their furs to Keelshies, some built and loaded their own canoes. Once the scouts reported that the river ice had broken, the group pushed off, waved away by those who stayed behind.

By this time, Keelshies had gathered enough canoes and furs, Shenan thought, to be chief for the day.

Just as Shenan had witnessed the geese in these northern lands alight in swampy grass only to depart in a matter of days, the Chipewyans, in just two moons, would leave Prince of Wales Fort. The process would reverse, the title of chief would be lost. Shed and dissolve, the band melting away, at the lakeshore, into the woods, across the plains, returning to their own families and winter grounds.

Keelshies wouldn't outright kill Waawaatee. No. Once his silly captain hat and English flag were packed deep in his pack and his band of followers, following themselves. Then, he would simply abandon her. Waawaatee would wake to hear an oar break the water or the sand as the last canoe pushed off. And he would leave her with tent and blanket, taking her cooking pot and bowl.

"We will be last in line, and only the daft Englishmen, who know no better, will see our furs," Shenan had whispered to Waawaatee the night before.

Waawaatee had merely nodded in agreement.

A heavy wooden board was removed from the window into the trading room, or "hole in the wall," as Shenan heard it referred to the previous night at dinner. The warehouse keeper stuck his head out, assessed the women, and then stepped back to reveal, to Shenan's surprise, Chief Keelshies.

Shenan had not known he would be in the trading room. She looked at Waawaatee and turned to leave the line. The old woman returned her gaze, defiant and cold, and stayed the girl with her hand. Waawaatee had known; of course she had known that Keelshies would be in the trading room. She had been to Prince of Wales Fort many times.

This would be perceived as an inexcusable affront and embarrassment—Keelshies's own women in possession of such fine furs that rightly belonged to him. The humiliation, tricked and fooled, the chief obviously not in control of his women.

Shenandoah had witnessed the chief's resentment toward Waawaatee grow and heave, like the ice in these Northern rivers. Just as the river ice would break in the spring, with a deafening noise like thunder and a rush of water, Keelshies's dislike for Waawaatee felt poised to burst. Shenan inched forward, bracing for Keelshies's wrath.

VII

Jeremiah's head was full of fog, and his neck hurt. He had not slept all night and was now bent over rows of figures, poised to record trades.

Keelshies took the furs from the women through the hole in the wall. The furs were assessed by the warehouse keeper and Governor Norton, then assigned a value in relation to one made beaver.

"One-fifth made beaver," the warehouse keeper would say.

Bricker, pale and unwell but present and standing, would translate the value.

Keelshies would shake his head and counter.

"One-fourth made beaver," Bricker would translate.

Norton and the warehouse keeper would nod and agree, this trade inconsequential and, as Jeremiah had learned, more a charity. These defective hides and furs would fetch next to nothing in London, but it was the trading ritual and custom. The chief and governor would settle on a meager amount, and the women would walk away with one or two made beaver in goods. Jeremiah meticulously recorded two ounces of beads or just one looking glass, two mere fishhooks, or a scanty awl.

Jeremiah saw the women light up when handed their little bundles, and he couldn't help a small smile as he dipped his pen in the inkwell and scratched the parchment with his numbers.

He was recording the last sale when he heard the warehouse keeper pronounce, "One made beaver."

Jeremiah looked up to see the slave girl and an old woman standing at the hole in the wall while the governor inspected a sleek ermine fur with black-tipped tail. Bricker had left his post next to Keelshies and was admiring the fur, calling it "a fine specimen."

Keelshies said something sharp to the women. The girl looked troubled, while the old woman held the chief with a steely stare. Keelshies spoke to Bricker, who translated, saying, "The chief says these furs do not belong to these women. And he fears, Governor, they were stolen."

"I trapped them," said the translator slave girl.

Keelshies again spoke to the women, his tone low and angry.

Jeremiah watched the governor, who held the ermine fur like a prize. A large bundle could be seen on the girl's back, and the governor's eyes rested upon it.

"Let us inspect the furs that she has brought. You may recognize them as stolen or missing. In the slight chance that she trapped these herself, having no husband to claim them, I presume ownership of said furs would fall to you, Chief Keelshies."

Bricker translated, and Keelshies seemed satisfied. The girl's mouth was in a tight line, and the old woman began to chant something softly. Keelshies eyed her nervously.

The remaining furs in the pack were similarly high quality. The governor gave a price of fifteen made beaver, a large amount considering the other women had traded to the amount of around one to two made beaver. Jeremiah recorded the value and looked helplessly at the girl in the window, who stood miserable and dejected. The old woman, however, continued to fix her eyes on Keelshies and mutter something low and rhythmic.

"Shall we add that to your account, Chief?" asked the warehouse keeper.

The chief eyed the old woman, her gaze pointed and unwavering, and even Jeremiah found her chanting unnerving. Keelshies spoke, his voice high-pitched and shaky. Bricker translated, saying, "Keelshies says these furs are insignificant to him. He has furs of great value, and the whores can have their wares."

The women traded the furs for a thick wool blanket, cooking pot, oatmeal, awl, sewing needles, thread, ice chisel, firesteel and hatchet. Jeremiah bundled the items. As he slid the sewing needles into a wooden box, his fingers migrated toward the Chinese beads and he edged in a handful before sliding on the lid.

Shenandoah had recriminations on her tongue, accusations as plentiful as the trade goods that were now piled in their small tent. The old woman was sitting quietly; she had opened the box of sewing needles and found an assortment of cylindrical light blue beads. She laid them on a moose fur.

Waawaatee took out her satchel, which contained objects pertaining to her position as a healer and spiritual guide. She removed three eagle feathers from the bag and laid them around her.

Shenan wanted to rail at the old crone, her own opportunity to serve the governor's daughter now fraught and tenuous. She was certain that she had looked troublesome and willful, trading furs without her master's permission.

Instead, Shenan sighed and asked, "Why have you arranged those eagle feathers so?"

"The eagle travels and speaks to the Great Spirit, Nitosi, and I ask the eagle to carry him a message."

"The message to kill Keelshies before he kills you?" asked Shenan, her resentment revealing itself.

"One would not ask the eagle to deliver that type of message to the Great Spirit," responded Waawaatee as she took a needle and thread and strung one blue bead. "The eagles communicate unselfish acts to the Creator. You were generous of Spirit, and the eagles will tell him so."

"Oh yes?" asked Shenan rudely. "How so?"

"Keelshies's eldest wife came here while you were fetching water this morning. The chief of the stone fort wants to buy you."

The old woman began to sew the beads in a straight, tight row at the bottom of her satchel. With the addition of each bead, she ran her fingers over the smooth line and crevices between.

"You have been generous with your labor and loyalty. You put yourself at risk by trading the furs when you no longer needed the goods."

Shenan put her head back and looked at the tent's low roof, full sun on the moose hide, shafts of light around the space. Her heart felt heavy as though tied to a bag of stones.

"Well, I suppose I didn't want to feel responsible for your death," countered Shenan, her eyes stinging. Since she had met Waawaatee, the old woman had been solid as rock and present as air. These two years, they had been like two rabbits asleep in a den, huddled for warmth and comforted by the rhythmic rise and fall of the other's breathing.

"I've never told you the story of my ancestor, the powerful sorceress who destroyed the Northern copper mine," said Waawaatee.

Shenan shook her head, no. Waawaatee was too wise to rise to her anger. Shenan sighed in defeat and said, "Last night at dinner, they spoke of one from Prince of Wales Fort, who has gone to look for this mine."

Waawaatee finished the bead border and set down the bag. From a small pouch she took out and inspected a handful of long, fine porcupine quills. "One of my ancestors, many generations ago, knew how to arrive at the mine. She led groups of men to this place, but she was the only woman in the party. They abused her and used her poorly. One trip, she cursed the men and their mine; she sat upon the mounds of metal and refused to leave."

Waawaatee chose a few quills and laid them on the moose fur. She then picked up and admired one of the blue beads, rotating it in the light.

With a small, pleased smile, the old woman said, "That young man must have slipped these into the box."

Yes, Shenan recognized him as the same person with the ill-fitting footman uniform, the one who expostulated after her speech—poor manners where Shenandoah came from. Effective speeches were followed by silence, to show respect and to reflect on the words.

"Your ancestor, did the men find her body? When they came back to the mine?" Shenan asked.

"Oh yes, they found her. She was in the same spot they had left her, alive and buried to her waist. The principal part of the mine was gone."

Waawaatee carefully lifted a quill from the moose hide, fragile as a piece of hay that snaps like a bone when dry. She dipped the quill into a pot of water that sat at the tent door and had warmed in the sun. She used one of her sewing needles to poke a small hole in the quill then pushed out the air until it resembled a flat ribbon. She began to add to the already intricate triangular quill design at the bag's center.

"And she stayed that way, half-buried?"

"No," said Waawaatee. "The next year, she was gone. And the copper mine was barren."

Shenan remembered the curses that Waawaatee had murmured and chanted at Keelshies in the trading room, unsettling him: "I will sink in the lake and destroy all the fish. I will lower into the earth and kill all the grass. I will ascend to the sky and put out the sun."

In their small tent, Waawaatee continued, "Keelshies and many other people in the tribe believe that I possess the power, through my ancestor, to take the source of their lives, just as she took the copper. I have never used this before in my favor."

After a long silence, Waawaatee continued, "Keelshies made promises to his father, concerning me, and they have protected me for as long as they will. I will be gone before the canoes depart."

Shenan had so many questions. Who was Keelshies's father? Why did his father care about Waawaatee? And, how did Waawaatee propose to pack and transport a tent and canoe worth of trade goods without the entire camp taking notice? Before she could ask these questions, Keelshies's brother made his presence known outside the tent door.

"The governor wants to speak with the slave."

At nine years old, Shenan had accompanied Uncle Andrew to Fort Stanwix for treaty negotiations. At this point, his bright star had faded, his scarlet damask waistcoat now shabby and stained with most likely vomit and gin. Long past were the days when he was sought by men the likes of Colonel Washington. When Uncle Andrew was drunk, which was nightly, and dancing or reminiscing around the fire, he would slur the words Washington had written: "Send me Montour. He would be of singular use to me here at this moment." Unable to read, Uncle had not read the letter, but Washington himself had told Uncle Andrew what he wrote, and implored, nay beseeched him to use his talents to aid the English. At least this was the story in Uncle Andrew's telling. These has been his glory days, and he had a particular affinity for this Washington man. Though, by the Treaty of Fort Stanwix the colonel no longer sent messengers and Uncle Andrew had lost his light.

Uncle Andrew had once negotiated his interpreting services for a new suit of clothes, thirty pistols, and 1,000 acres of land, a princely sum. Shenan imagined him at this time, his ever-present black cordovan scarf tied round his neck and decked with small silver bugles. Now the scarf hung limp, threads where missing charms once dangled, those that remained, tarnished and rusted.

Meme had just died, hence why Shenan followed Uncle Andrew to Fort Stanwix. Both of them were wounded birds with clipped wings, holes in their hearts where Meme had lived. Shenan was now in the care of her uncle and too young to understand why the only person who had protected, cared for, clothed, and loved her was gone. She looked up, the last leaves of the season letting go of the trees. The sky, Meme's heaven, was grey like the barrel of a gun. Shenan still wasn't sure if Meme came back from there or stayed.

On this trip, one man gave her sweets and a little rag doll wearing a calico dress. Another man gave her a spinning top while leaning close to her face, patting her head. As instructed, she danced for them around the fire.

"Who does the squaw belong to?" asked one fur trader with rotten teeth and a filthy suit of clothes that looked as stiff as bark.

"I suppose me, now, gentlemen," Uncle Andrew said, his eyes like dead flat plates. Since Meme's death, he seemed only to put one foot in front of the other. The men exchanged loaded looks, and Shenan felt as though a spider crawled up her back.

They made her drink brandy, and her throat burned.

She woke in the pitch darkness as a man pinned her to the ground. No idea which man, could have been any number of them, clumsy and inebriated. He shifted awkwardly to undo his belt, and she heard the twang of the clasp.

Thankfully, in Uncle Andrew's grief or laziness, or need to start drinking, he hadn't properly secured the sides of their tent. As the man struggled to pull down his undergarments, he fell to the side, cursing, and she took the opportunity to slip out like a field mouse disappears beneath a rock.

She ran with the howling wind at her back and rain coming down in sheets. Eventually, she settled into a patch of wet moss.

Sleeping outside in the icy rain, curled around herself and soaked to the bone, was perhaps the moment, Shenan reflected, when she started to understand the world.

By the time the governor asked for Shenandoah, she no longer danced for men.

Waawaatee said, "Let the chief of the stone fort pretend you're the hare and he's the fox, but you're actually watching from above, the hawk." Keelshies's brother, already walking, turned around and spoke to her sharply. Shenan could not respond, but the words gave her courage.

She had every intention of acting proper, demure, and timid, but had considered her value. Rumor in the camp was that the governor's daughter lived at Prince of Wales Fort. Shenan had observed the Fort's interior and exterior and grasped its complete isolation. She was most certainly one of the only females who knew the ways of the English that would ever set foot on this frozen rock.

She followed a company man into the Fort and through the courtyard to the governor's house. She was led into an office where the governor sat behind an enormous wooden desk, head bent over parchment with the names of trade goods and figures. "The surgeon," as they called him, was beside the bookcase, which contained rows of books bound in green buckram with dark red leather spines.

The governor was scratching numbers onto the parchment with the shaft of a feather he used as a quill. Without taking his eyes off his figures, he said, "We don't believe the story that you are a relative of the Montours. Nor have we heard of them."

He then looked up, leaned forward, and forced eye contact. She understood the look to mean, *And don't go on about it, your fabricated ancestry.*

The surgeon coughed uncomfortably, and his fingers fumbled to remove a book from the shelf, which he opened awkwardly. While looking down, he said, "Problem is, child, you were abandoned to voyageurs and—"

"You are another orphaned and abandoned Native child," interrupted the governor. "A valued Native child wouldn't have been so deserted."

Shenan's throat filled at his biting discernment and the truth of his words.

"Regardless of how you got here, or where you came from, you are the first girl to arrive at the Bay with any knowledge of English life or, for that matter, the English language. Except, of course, for my daughter, Mary, who has been taught and taught well."

The governor said this last sentence with an air of defensive pride, and Shenan intuited this as a weakness, the first that she had seen from this man. She said nothing but stored away this knowledge like the cracks running through the stone behind him.

"If you would like to leave in a few days with the chief," and the Governor's mouth twisted in a subtle, cruel smile, "you are welcome. If you would like to stay here and work for me, caring for my daughter and any other tasks that I may require of you . . ." He drifted off.

"Would I be a slave?" Shenan asked, and knew that she was taking a risk. She should accept the offer and not anger this man who she sensed was, at heart, a snake.

However, she had not known until she became a slave what it meant. To be free and live, perhaps not the life of an English lady or Native princess, but the life of a Native girl, with a connected family, and then to be owned, and at the will of other people. To eat only when others were full to the point of vomiting. To sleep under either no blanket or one riddled with holes and vermin. To be regarded as not a life and the first to die. She'd like to call the experience humbling, but it actually just made her angry. And this was a negotiation. As much as Governor Norton wanted to stare her down with his dark and dangerous eyes, she knew his type—the semblance of power, authority, and demands, all tottering on shifting spring ice. Powerful men fell fast and quick, if Meme had taught her nothing else.

"You would be taken, to start, as a servant," Governor Norton said shortly. He resumed studying the figures, his fingers hovered around the quill and his eyes ran back and forth along the trade goods and numbers on the page.

Shenan was purchased for a few guns, some yards of scarlet linen cloth that Keelshies's beautiful wife had coveted, and a generous amount of Brazil tobacco. Before she left the room, the governor commented that his daughter, Mary, was a proper lady. If he noted any corrupting influence, Shenan would be traded back next season. Shenan left, with head down and shuffling feet, so the governor would believe she was under the heel of his shoe. And she gave him a wide-eyed, scared look so he would believe that he was in control. But all the while, she remembered the words of Waawaatee and imagined her spirit above the Fort, circling the sky as a hawk, scanning the Bay for the ship that would take her back. Back to somewhere.

VIII

Jeremiah had not understood that the blue beads were more valuable than the other trade beads. There were fewer of them, apparently; the ones on the table were the entire supply. They lay out for the purpose that Keelshies might take notice. As Jeremiah learned in the mess hall, the London Committee would be sending no more and were eager to be rid of them. The Chinese blue beads had been sitting these three years with no interest from the Natives. Now, half the beads in the box were gone, and no one had paid for them. Stolen.

"One pound of Chinese beads is worth six made beaver, while the company beads go only for two," said the mason in the mess hall that evening. Jeremiah had shown up after graciously allowed a nap, awake as he'd been a day and a half. And the beads that he had taken were the topic of conversation.

"The company will be happy to be rid of them," continued the mason. "By my word, the beads are of no matter. It'll be the theft, the act of it!"

Per the retelling, the warehouse keeper hadn't even needed to count them, to exclaim, "Someone's been in the Chinese beads!" Jeremiah had thankfully missed this and was quite certain if present he would have revealed himself, inept as he was at hiding guilt.

The warehouse keeper had dismissed him before the theft was discovered. His eyes were shutting, his head almost hitting the account book. "Jeremiah," the keeper had said sharply, "go lie down a spell."

As he walked out, he heard the man say in a softer tone, "The boy was at it all night, on watch."

Back in the mess hall, Jeremiah was now bent over his plate, kindly prepared for him by the cooper, though yet again missing his biscuit.

The armourer said, "Must have been that Chipewyan chief."

"Still, he's been shown those blue beads other seasons and never cared for them," said the tailor, sounding dubious. "Would the man not take a little tobacco or shot?"

The carpenter declared, "If those of us due to go home next year don't receive our token of appreciation because of suspicion over some damned blue beads!"

Those men expected home on next year's ship all murmured agreement.

During mess hall evenings, Jeremiah learned that the London Committee encouraged the governors to know their advantage. Officially, a gun was worth ten made beaver, but if the Natives would trade it for twelve or fifteen, that was all the better. As the powder was poured into the horn, or shot tapped into the pouch, the warehouse keeper or governor might say to the man preparing the goods, "Easy there, son," or "I'd say that's about right." A little off the top was "overplus," and overplus trickled down. First, the creditors; second, next year's operation; third, dividends for the investors; and last, bonuses, gifts, a mark of favor from the committee to their employees in the Bay—a few guineas, a pocket watch, a fine tea set, a silver tray, something the men could keep or more likely sell.

Jeremiah tried to look engrossed in the fish and turnip before him as the men in the mess hall now debated who had been present in the trading room.

Counting off on fingers, they mentioned Chief Keelshies, Daniel Bricker, the warehouse keeper, Governor Norton, and that boy Jeremiah.

"Hospital Kid!" bellowed one of the laborers from the Orkneys. "What did you see?"

Before he could answer, the gunner called out, "Bleeding Heart!" using a new nickname that Jeremiah had acquired after his outburst for the slave girl. "Did you take notice of the beads at the start of trade?"

Jeremiah stared down at his plate and mumbled, "To be honest, I was so fatigued from night watch. And it being my first time keeping the accounts . . ." He drifted off.

"For sure, they are rolling in the pocket of some sailor, as we speak, almost out of the Bay and halfway to England!" pronounced the armourer.

This statement met with approval, murmurs of "crooked seaman" and "damned mariners." By now, Jeremiah was familiar with the mess hall resentment toward the sailors who were paid more than the Bay men. And he was grateful that attention moved from him to this longstanding foe.

"The warehouse keeper swears, as do Bricker and the governor, that the blue beads were there and accounted for at the commencement of trade."

This was said by Francis Moncrief, master of the sloop that traded yearly with the Esquimaux at a place called Marble Island. Moncrief came to the Bay a carpenter and shipbuilder, Jeremiah had learned, though early on revealed himself a master of many trades and rose through the ranks. Now an officer, he was expected to eat in the dining room but could often be found in the mess hall. Jeremiah wasn't sure if the man merely preferred the company of the laborers or had been instructed to keep an eye and handle on those "below stairs." However, from Jeremiah's observations, those "above stairs" also merited their own close watching.

Moncrief continued, "I agree with you men. The beads are of no importance in terms of profit, yet the theft will cast suspicion. It must go reported and occurred with a Native in the trading room and in the presence of two officers. The London Committee's concerns will, as usual, be misplaced but present nonetheless."

Following the sloop master's speech came a resigned silence. The men looked glum, and the cooper began taking morose sips from Jeremiah's beer, his own being dry.

"Well," started the armourer again, "if they were stolen, they'll suspect us all, as they are wont to do, and I won't be getting a timepiece or set of china or whatever damned useless thing they were going to gift me. And to think all the men thieving and robbing in this place and all they will concern themselves with are some trifling beads!"

"Me held accountable, when it had to be one of the men in that room!" yelled the gunner.

So that was that. Jeremiah was a suspect, and in the moment he hadn't even given the act a second thought. He had wanted to give the girl and old woman something. He could feel their desperation and admired the old woman's ferocity, her resolve.

When the warehouse keeper asked, "Should we add that to your account, Chief Keelshies?" Jeremiah's heart felt wounded for the girl and old woman, their labors and effort, unpaid, unappreciated, taken by some Indian chief who had plenty when the girl and woman had rags and hungry eyes. The world was flat, round, crooked, straight, and in between. He had no other explanation than that giving those beads made it feel aright.

IX

As her first duty, Shenan was sent directly from the governor's office to Mary's room to dress her for dinner. She soon learned this was silly; she had no clue how to dress an English lady, and Mary had fared for years on her own. All Mary did, Shenan was soon to learn, she did to perfection.

Mary showed Shenan how to tighten the stays, hold the hoop as she stepped in, and lift the cream-colored bedgown, printed with blue floral sprays, over her head. She assisted Mary to pin the fine linen scarf embroidered with whitework of ovals and leaves.

Afterward, Mary, her eyes like deep brown windows, looked at Shenan and she felt swallowed by kindness. Mary had flawless golden skin, soft features, and a graceful body like a slender birch.

"I hope," Mary said, "we can be sisters. I have always dreamed of a sister." She kissed Shenan on the cheek and floated from the room, her footfall noiseless and her skirts with the faintest rustle.

Shenan was taking in her surroundings when the little man named John America entered. She was staring at the ornate four-poster bed which dominated the room, an imposing object with a paneled headboard and balusters decorated with floral carvings. The furniture was a polished walnut and the canopy a rich green and gold damask.

She had seen this boy around the Fort and at the dinner, running from the kitchens to the dining room with dishes for the footmen to serve.

"A pleasure to meet you," he said. He extended his hand, and she shook it.

"Mary has a lovely room," said the boy. He gestured toward the upholstered armchair and thick polar bear rug before the fireplace, the armoire, dressing table, and bookshelf. An impressive dollhouse was tucked in the corner.

Shenan nodded toward the bed. "Is this not where the governor's wife sleeps?"

"Oh no," said John America. "Father ordered Mary this bed a few years ago. And the governor's wife, she lives in England."

This boy referred to the governor as Father so he was apparently another child of that man. She wondered why this little mister wasn't sleeping in Mary's room as the governor's son. He wore a well-made suit of caribou hide decorated with tassels.

Shenan walked over to the dressing table and set down the pincushion she had used to affix Mary's bodice and scarf. This brought her beside the three-story dollhouse. The bottom floor was comprised of three rooms, the middle with a grand staircase and long dining table. To the left was a kitchen, the sort Shenan had glimpsed from the threshold of the finest homes in Philadelphia. It contained a brick fireplace and hearth, rows of wooden benches and tables for food preparation, and even tiny bowls with wooden apples and oranges. In the third room were tall windows, blue walls with gold trim, miniature paintings, gold-gilded furniture, and a crystal chandelier. The second and third floors boasted bedroom upon bedroom, with variations of four-poster beds hung with scarlet velvet and white floral linen and even one bed hung with a green and gold damask identical to that on Mary's bed.

John America said, "Father hopes Mary will be mistress of a house like that one day. But," he lowered his voice, "Mary says she never will. She is betrothed." He broke into a wide smile. "She's promised to

Samuel Hearne. Have you heard of him?"

Shenan shook her head, unsure at first, and then remembered. "Yes, the man who is looking for the copper mine." The mine, Shenan thought, that Waawaatee's ancestor destroyed.

"Yes, the same," said the boy. "He is very good to Mary and," with his voice so low it was now a whisper, "they've made promises to one another."

Shenan had witnessed many White men make promises to young women like Mary but didn't have the heart to tell this friendly boy that those promises weren't promises at all.

"I am so pleased that Mary will have a companion," John America said. "Excuse me, they will be looking for me in the kitchens." And the boy was gone.

At his departure, the room became so quiet, Shenan could hear the walls cracking as though the stone was shifting. She became aware that she was, yet again, in another unfamiliar world—Meme, Uncle Andrew, Keelshies, and now this Governor Norton with his, at first impression, lovely daughter. Shenan had a new set of rules to learn, assume, appropriate, and pretend to live by.

She felt exhausted. The armchair in front of the fire looked soft and deep, but she settled upon the polar bear rug and added a few sticks of wood to the fire, thinking the governor would not want Mary to be cold. She inspected the polar bear's head, his yellow teeth, and grey tongue. He looked as if he were screaming and did not want to die. The head was terrifying, but the fur was luxurious. Killed in the dead of winter, Shenan supposed, when his coat was at its thickest.

The next morning, Mary told Shenan that she found her asleep before the fire lying on, what turned out to be, the governor's prized polar bear rug. Mary had covered her with a linen sheet and wool blanket, which Shenan found heaped upon her as the morning light snuck in the solitary window and the fire was spent to ash.

X

Jeremiah and Rodney were appointed, until further notice and indefinitely, to second night watch.

Rodney claimed he was an owl by nature and had stood watch in his London parish of Ratcliffe, over merchant's warehouses and captain's docked ships.

Jeremiah learned that Rodney was in fact considered a dedicated employee who due to age and infirmity was not serviceable for hauling wood, mending walls, or any sort of serious hunting. He was to receive thirty pounds a year and be given small tasks as befit his station. Rodney slipped easily into the role of second night watch not of use for much else except to tell war stories and carry light loads. His back, he proclaimed to all who would listen, was as old as the *Prince Rupert*, the boat he arrived on twenty years before that was now driftwood floating on the Thames.

The "old" man, if he deserved the appellation, was profiting hand over fist from this assignment. Officer and laborer alike sneaking out or their women in, handing Rodney a little this or that, the clink of a coin in hand. The scoundrel, head inclined, would demur, "Mum's the word, much obliged."

Rodney was making his fortune out in his wooden chair, the air so silent, one could depend on it.

"I'm going to train you, boy," he said, leaning in close. "You can earn a living for a wife and child or that mother and sister of yours. You won't be going back with gold bangles down your arms, like the East India boys, but you can retire a comfortable old man."

He continued, "I'll tell the governor that in two days' time, I'm taking you out to show you a few tricks of trapping and such before winter sets in."

"I would appreciate that, Rodney," said Jeremiah, sincerely. He had seen nothing of this country, and the company paid half to the employee what the fur fetched when sold in London. This might be his only opportunity to supplement his meager apprentice wage for Mother and Agnes. He was sure that their gloves were worn and darned to pieces by now. They probably wore the same dresses he had seen them in two years ago.

Before morning watch arrived, Jeremiah and Rodney set out as planned. Jeremiah was surprised to head first toward a pile of rubbish, rotten staves, rusted hoops, and discarded stone piled up outside the walls. Rodney started hauling out vials of brandy, rolls of tobacco, cloth, beads, and even a kettle—everything Jeremiah had seen Rodney bribed with at the door and more.

"Put these in your pack," Rodney hissed. He started handing Jeremiah the goods. Jeremiah began to sweat and glanced over his shoulder, up the ramparts, into the sky and out to sea.

He now understood why Rodney had picked the hatchet and file out of his pack and said, "Won't need that, leave that," but left Jeremiah's small heirloom knife and said, "This might fetch something." Jeremiah suspected they wouldn't be setting traps.

The two were well across the tundra and out of sight with their conspicuous bundles before they heard the low beat of the drum, rousing the men to breakfast and the day's work.

Jeremiah inhaled the pure air and released a long breath. It was as though two stones of weight dropped from his shoulders. He had been living in a state of perpetual anxiety. The officers and other men teased him mercilessly; were they indeed tormenting and terrorizing him, or was it just good fun? He felt like he couldn't say a word or take a step without tripping.

The sunrise was a brilliant orange, and the grass waved with an easy ocean breeze. Spreads of a purple pink flower reminded Jeremiah of the foxglove back home, rolling over the ground like a blanket. There was a white flower, shaped like a cup, that reminded him of the wild orchid back home.

The land stretched forever before him, and Jeremiah thought again of the maps at the company's office in London, with their blurred white edges of an undiscovered world. Formations of geese flew overhead, and birds sprang from the grass. For the first time since he'd left England, he felt the open space before him. The dark stone walls of Prince of Wales Fort were a prison. This was freedom except for the mosquitos, which swarmed his eyes, ears, and mouth like an angry miniature army. Already his arms rose with knots and bumps from their bites.

Would he ever go home, to England? He left there for a reason. He was not successful there, and he was not successful here. In England he had thought, if only I were somewhere else, then I'd be right, I'd be someone. Here at Prince of Wales Fort, nothing had changed. He felt exactly the same. In the mess hall in the evening, awake in his bed, during those long endless nights on watch, he found himself thinking again, if only I were somewhere else, I'd be someone.

At the end of today, he and Rodney would walk back through the Fort gates. But did he have to? He could just keep walking. He wanted no walls, the walls he was inside and those that people put around him. He wanted to look ahead at something clear, open, and of his own creation. This wilderness had no expectation of him, nor he of it, and in that space there was a future, a place to lose oneself and, if he wanted, not be found.

He and Rodney walked a few hours before they came upon a clump of spruce, a tree island in the midst of the tundra, the dense branches of which Rodney entered at random. At least it so appeared to Jeremiah, but he soon realized they were on a path. When he thought they were coming out the other side, they emerged into a clearing with five moose hide tents, taut and snug over poles that stuck out the top.

Rodney set course toward the largest of the five tents and ducked in. Jeremiah followed and took a moment to adjust his eyes. Coals glowed in a center ring of stones, the smoke curling toward the tent's top and out the hole but also dispersing throughout, creating a grey and cloudy air. Around the fire sat a few Elder men. At the back facing the opening appeared to be the patriarch or leader of this camp, introduced by Rodney as Segenam.

Segenam wore no shirt, and though it was August and the tent was warm, a voluminous beaver cape was tied at his neck, draped over his shoulders, and spread around him in waving folds.

He invited Rodney to sit beside him, and as Rodney picked his way carefully around the Elders, he said to Jeremiah, "Sit by the door. The unmarried sit by the door." Jeremiah sat directly by the flap and was continuously hit with it as men and women, young and old, and children, all filed in until the tent was so brim-full not another soul could fit.

Rodney opened his pack and cut a thumb's worth off his roll of Brazil tobacco, which Segenam accepted graciously. The pipe was started and passed until spent. The trading then commenced.

Rodney did not speak the language but knew a sort of sign language.

"I wouldn't go trying to learn the language," Rodney had told Jeremiah on the way. "First off, where did that get Bricker? Mark my words. Norton isn't done with him yet. Besides, the Natives around the Bay, they speak one language; you walk two hours, they speak another."

Rodney laid out his treasures, and the children were sent to a wooden structure of hewn logs at the edge of camp, the cracks caulked with moss and mud. They came back with bundles of marten furs. An interval ensued of good-natured haggling, or so it appeared to Jeremiah. Rodney made use of his hands to communicate through signs and replenish the pipe with more knots from his roll.

He and Jeremiah walked away with twenty marten furs.

Not before, however, Segenam had offered Rodney a young woman who sat so far back and tucked in the corner that through the smoke Jeremiah could barely distinguish her features.

Rodney made some motions to his back and other signs, which appeared to amuse the men and women in the tent.

Segenam then gestured to Jeremiah, who realized in horror that she was now offered to him. Through a brief clearing of smog, he caught sight of the young woman's impassive and unreadable expression. He turned scarlet red. Was he expected to take the woman right here? Would they go into one of the neighboring tents? He had never been with a woman.

"She doesn't, Rodney, look willing," Jeremiah hissed.

"It's no matter, boy. The women here are of sundry sort." Rodney waved his hand dismissively. "Besides, Segenam will be insulted."

Silence swelled in the tent, and Jeremiah could hear a roaring in his ears. He scanned the faces around him and felt his entire body tingle with panic. It was unbearably hot. The smoke was irritating his eyes and choking his throat. Rodney made a quick succession of signs, and the tent erupted in laughter. Jeremiah shot a quick glance at the young woman, who, he couldn't help but notice, looked relieved.

After many bows of the head and respectful gestures, he and Rodney ducked out of the tent. As they left, children skipped beside them and from his pouch Rodney produced spinning tops, which he placed in each outstretched hand. The children accompanied them out of the clearing and into the wood until shouts were heard from camp, their mothers calling to them. The children turned on heel and, gripping their prizes, skipped merrily back the way they had come.

Jeremiah was too distracted and humiliated on the walk back to the Fort to notice the beauty around him. He was incapable of contemplation or the feeling of release that he had on the way to the Native camp. Rodney seemed content to walk along in silence, his usual tales and lectures absent.

So buried in his own thoughts, he didn't notice that Rodney took a turn on the tundra away from the Fort. Jeremiah now found himself staring at the sea, standing on rocks that rolled over the land as if they were lounging or sleeping.

This was Button Bay, and though Jeremiah couldn't see it, he knew the Fort lay to the southeast, on that same visible outcropping of land that was called Esquimaux Point.

Rodney signaled Jeremiah over to help him roll a large stone that sat in front of a rock crevice. A dry crawl space was revealed, and the walls inside bore signs of a chisel.

"Empty now, boy. The captain just cleaned me out." Rodney smiled and shook his head back and forth as though his prized children had just been sold and he was happy about it. "Is it really fair with the low wages we are paid to give half our profits to the company?" He paused, and Jeremiah knew he was supposed to agree, but when he did not, Rodney carried on undeterred. "The sailors and captains take a little something, still more than their share—thieves. But then I do as I please. No company tracking my earnings, deciding I need to spend it on that York Native woman who claims she has some child by me."

Rodney gave a contented sigh and looked around Button Bay at his little cave warehouse and the tundra behind, like a man taking stock of his dominion. "I need to spend a day down here and chisel out more space before I fill her up again."

Jeremiah was then tasked with pushing the bundles to the far reaches of Rodney's spot, accomplished only by getting on his stomach and scratching himself to pieces as he pushed the bundles as far back as they would go.

"I'll give you a little something for your trouble," Rodney assured him. "I'd be laid up a week with this back if I did that."

As they walked along the rocks back to the tundra, Rodney said,

"You can thank me another time for my help with the Natives." Jeremiah snorted. This man was truly unbelievable. "For my part, I told them I suffered the gravel and stone, you know, the painful urination. I haven't taken a woman since a few years back at York when I got the venereal distemper. When that happens," he said, wagging a finger Jeremiah's way, who wanted to point out he'd never had such a thing, "you'll be paying a month's wages to the surgeon for the cure. Remember that."

"So you wanted me to get the distemper?" Jeremiah retorted, which Rodney for some reason found humorous and let out a low chuckle.

"You know, son, this has been a good day for me. A good day."

They were quiet again as they walked, and Jeremiah craved the release he had felt when they first left the Fort. It had been a balm for his soul—a soul confused and discouraged since landing on these shores. But now all he saw was the girl. Her skin had gleamed like dark, polished wood and her shirt, though not immodest, was tight over her breasts. He felt ashamed but couldn't stop his mind from imagining her entire body, naked.

He felt on fire and fell behind Rodney as though he wanted space, worried that the cunning devil would somehow read his thoughts. As much as he tried, he couldn't stop imagining his hand running up her skin and their bodies hot and pressed together.

XI

Shenandoah was to care for Mary, though in actuality, Mary took care of herself and everyone else. Mary's greatest challenge, Shenan was to learn, was her father.

Mary didn't haul wood and water, pluck geese, or dress skins. She was not allowed. As winter took hold, Mary's task, which she did with quiet determination and grace, was to keep those around her from disintegrating from depression and despair. Her steadfast faith, calm presence, and accepting way were a source of solace and comfort. Sometimes it worked. Other times, it was not enough to keep the endless ice and brutal cold from thwarting the men's minds, their glassy eyes hiding thoughts that ran as far as the horizon and as deep as the sea.

The men were constantly together. The windows were no longer just glass but blocks of ice and frost. A ceramic mug of water that sat right next to the fire froze solid and cracked. One laborer was sent to fetch wood and was brought back the next morning carried by three men like a log, his body the color of the fish they ate at dinner. Tempers ran as short as a Hudson Bay summer.

A soothing and encouraging word from Mary, her salve on a black and swollen eye, a small gift purchased from the warehouse with her allowance to raise up a breaking spirit, or even just her fervent, "You are in my thoughts and prayers"—this made the Fort inhabitants feel right. It made Shenan feel, even if she was not right, that she would always be right with Mary.

The governor needed this most. Shenan came to learn that his terrorizing exterior was the cover of a deranged and paranoid man, a man plagued with the thought that on the next ship a letter would arrive from the London Committee. It had come to their attention that he was the son of a Cree woman, not the Englishwoman Susan as he claimed, and it was against policy for Natives to hold contract positions in the company. He would be handed this letter by his replacement, his prestigious and coveted position gone.

Mary's room sat at the end of the hall in a corner of the governor's house. Her bedroom door sat slightly ajar, the light from the fire and candles sending a light down the cold and dreary passageway. Even in the cruelest of weather, Shenan, Governor Norton, John America, and later, Samuel Hearne, could rely on that strip of light; Mary never completely shut the door except to sleep, and the warm beams were a beacon in their times of need.

As Shenan neared Mary's room, she always knew when the governor was inside; his voice alternated between low and high hysteria, staccato sounds as his mind released into words the imagined plots of his enemies. She would plaster her body against the far wall, side step just beyond that beam of light, and work her way to the back side of the door. She was waiting for him to leave so she could sit with Mary. While thus absconded, she learned more than she wanted to know about Mary's disturbed and crazy father.

The rant was always the same. If Governor Norton fooled London and they continued to want to be fooled, how could he tolerate these men? Every employee, laborer, and officer alike, every sailor, fresh off the boat, they eyed and flirted with his women. In his office, when he entertained the trading parties and officers at dinner, while he was sleeping; behind the walls and outside the Fort and in the blacksmith shop, the kitchen, the warehouse, they were all fornicating and carrying on. With his women. If he were an Englishman, no one would dare touch them. And these damn bastards, stealing from him. Stealing from the company, affecting his overplus, dragging his name through the mud. No, he would find this copper, silver, gold. He would figure out the Northwest Passage once and for all. And there would be no discussion, no debate about where he came from.

These were the things the governor said to Mary as he reclined on her bed and she sat beside him, holding his hand, singing to calm him. Or he sat in the chair staring at the fire, ranting and gesturing wildly while Mary sat on a stool at his side, her cheek resting on his arm and listening.

The governor either didn't care where Shenan was, or believed, as Mary told him, that Shenan was darning the petticoat, scrubbing Spurrell's careless wine out of Mary's silk, or embroidering tiny flowers on a handkerchief border. So, while Governor Norton thought Shenan was with the tailor or at the laundry or plucking a goose in the kitchen, which she sometimes was doing, she was oftentimes waiting impatiently behind Mary's door.

She, like everyone else in Mary's small circle, wanted to sit in safety on the polar bear rug and read books aloud while the young woman worked at her sewing or embroidery. John America would sometimes be there. He whittled a piece of wood or played with his spinning top and marbles. Sometimes, he sifted through the sewing needles and took out those with broken tips and inspected axe blades, files, and chisels for cracks or imperfections.

Mary spent a good deal of time embroidering her trousseau—MAH, Mary Anne Hearne—and she had chosen a light blue thread, the embroidery hoop holding the white linen taut, the letters an unadorned cursive, and, at the edges, light blue and yellow flowers that reminded Shenan of daisies. The pattern was simple and elegant. Her graceful head would be bent over this work, and Shenan would read. Mary only had a few approved volumes in her bookcase, and one was *The Young Gentleman and Lady Instructed in Such Principles of Politeness, Prudence, and Virtue.*

The governor would appear leaning against the doorframe and observe them. Mary, pushing her needle and thread carefully through the fine fabric, John America working on some project or another, and Mary's servant, as Shenan was sure the governor saw her, reading lines such as "A female library should consist of such authors, as do not corrupt, while they divert; but should tend more immediately to improve them, as they are women." The governor would shake his head and walk away with a content smile.

On clear days, Shenan and John America were sometimes sent to the shore to harvest mussels. During one such outing, he told her that Waawaatee was living one day's walk from the Fort. She had carved out her own little lair under the root system of a tree ripped from the ground during a winter storm.

"She looks well," John America said, as he pried the mussel off the rock and handed it to Shenan. "Her hut is quite cozy. She has laid branches lengthwise, and it is well caulked. I do not know her language, but she tolerates me and even has given me some oatmeal."

Shenan was beyond relieved to hear the old woman was alive.

Keelshies had set off that third morning, his uncle wearing the captain's hat and the Union Jack flying in the stern. Governor Norton was at the shore with a farewell gift of tobacco and brandy for the long trip home. The standards were snapping in the wind, and the drummers were trying to drum and hold on to their hats. Shenan was at the shore holding a bag of oatmeal, a gift from the governor to Keelshies's eldest wife.

Waawaatee was nowhere to be seen. In the canoe of Keelshies's beautiful wife, the stern was empty except for Waawaatee's moose hide tent in her seat. A bulge hinted where her new trading goods were presumed to be stored, which Keelshies was sure to take at the first opportunity. As the chief stood proudly, ready to push off and the ceremonial moment nigh, Keelshies's brother discreetly looked under the tent skins, and Shenan could see piles of moss and grass where the trade goods should have been. Keelshies's expression froze and he made no acknowledgment, as

Shenan was sure the insult of the fur sale had been enough, and now the old woman had tricked him and escaped. Shenan also knew his wives would pay for not keeping a closer eye on the old bat.

Keelshies's beautiful wife picked up an oar and plopped down in the stern like a small child on the brink of a tantrum. Shenan smiled even now at the memory, as this was perhaps one of the most satisfying moments of her life.

John America said Waawaatee lived in her den, as yet, without molestation, even breaking the fever of one of Governor Norton's cousins and applying a poultice to the angry wound of one of his nephews.

"I'm not sure, though, if the hunting is poor this winter that they will remain so kind," John America admitted as the pair headed back to the Fort with their basket of mussels.

Shenandoah knew this to mean that if a family was starving, Waawaatee, the stranger and her bundles, would be the first to go.

XII

Jeremiah had never experienced such cold. At night, he and Rodney dressed in every article of clothing they owned and were permitted a fire within a stone ring.

Jeremiah no longer felt compelled to walk the perimeter. He roamed the buildings in an aimless and haphazard manner. Sometimes, Rodney would send a friend to fetch him for some task or another, though his route and location could rarely be relied upon.

"Where were you, boy?" Rodney would hiss, holding some privately traded good as though it were burning his hand. He wanted it stashed quickly before he was caught with it.

Jeremiah now spent his nights dreaming. What more was there to do in those long hours when the governor was still awake entertaining his friends, his women? Jeremiah did, however, always know where he was headed when his watch first began. He went to the governor's window to hear Mary play the piano and listen to her sweet voice before she retired for the evening.

Rodney concurred, "That's Mary. She plays well. An officer taught her when her mother was still alive."

In his dreamlike state, Jeremiah didn't mention to Rodney that he thought there was a bird in the governor's rooms—that was until one night when he heard the bird clear and crisp while passing the governor's window, which was always obscured frustratingly with either condensation or frost.

"There's a parrot in the governor's rooms, I'm sure of it," Jeremiah told Rodney, expecting that Rodney would be as shocked as he was.

Rodney shot him a deprecating look. "You've just learned of the parrot?" Rodney held up his pinky finger, the tip missing.

Missing fingers, a scar or burn, and disfigurement of some kind were not uncommon amongst the Bay employees. Jeremiah had assumed Rodney had lost his finger with the ill swing of a hatchet or perhaps from frostbite.

"The parrot bit your finger?" asked Jeremiah, incredulous.

"That parrot is a bastard. If the governor asks you to pet it, say no. It eats fingers."

Jeremiah shuddered.

"What did the governor do?" asked Jeremiah.

Rodney looked him straight in the eye. "He laughed." He picked up his stick and revived their little fire. "He thought I was—this was a few years back—interested in one of his women. He wasn't wrong. To this day I know it was a warning. And," Rodney said, holding up his pinky and waving it about, "I took it seriously, though some idiots do not."

That fall, Segenam came at night to the small wooden door with a bundle of marten pelts, which Rodney traded for brandy.

Segenam invited Jeremiah to visit the camp and it was implied, his daughter. Rodney secured the governor's permission for the young man to check the imaginary traps that they had not made or set.

Jeremiah set out on a clear day, the sun just rising over the sea. He wore three pairs of stockings that reached almost clear to his waist, caribou hide britches, moccasins, and a double-lined waistcoat under which he wore every shirt he owned, covered by what was called a beaver toggy. The beaver cape, per Rodney, was valuable and sewn from ten quality beaver furs. He wore leather mittens lined inside and out with beaver fur, and when the wind whipped and penetrated even his face covering, he laid the beaver fur on his cheeks to keep them warm.

Rodney instructed him, "If you die out there, Governor Norton will list the only loss as that cape. So, if you anticipate you'll perish, secure it in a tree please, son."

Jeremiah wrapped the cape around his skinny frame. His face was covered with only a hole for the nose and eyes by something called a chin clout, topped with a flannel cap and a hood.

Rodney had produced the beaver toggy and told him he must wear it. "I've seen a man freeze to death not five hundred feet from the Fort before my very eyes. And not a man to save him for if they were to try, they would have perished just the same."

Jeremiah walked back toward the Fort many hours later, the sun now setting over the woods he had just departed. His socks and shoes had dried beside Segenam's fire while he spent a few hours, enjoyable for him, with Segenam's daughter.

Was she his woman, his "bit of brown"? No, he wouldn't call her that. The girl had, if anything, made him uneasy. He wasn't certain that she disliked him but quite certain she didn't like him. She didn't loath the experience, he thought, but she didn't enjoy it. Did she want him to come around a few more times? No, he decided, she'd be content to never see him again. In summary, she was unreadable, but he understood. He giggled, giddy from the experience, the crunch of snow under his feet. The cold air and the pink sky felt sharp and real.

After all, he didn't care. He had come for something, paid for it, and got it. That was the way and how these things went.

What had Rodney and the men in the mess hall been telling him all along? It was this easy. This place belonged to no one. There were no fences, rock walls, nor hedges. There were no castles nor estates. The Natives didn't act like kings nor dukes; they acted like your neighbor or friend. Was it wrong to take Segenam's daughter when she did not favor him? The Hudson's Bay Company, the king, he was sure, would not approve of fornication with non-Christians. Yet, they were not even as present as the stars. They wanted something—coin—and he wanted the same. How they got there, and how he got there, was a beautiful story they could all write down and a true story no one really had to tell.

What he wanted for Agnes and his mother were London apartments, well-appointed and overlooking a park, as well as servants and a carriage. Dresses for balls, afternoon walks, visiting hours with fine ladies, introductions to the right people and wealthy men. A dowry.

The gentlemen and ladies of London would ask, "And who is that girl? Who is her father?"

And someone would reply, "Her father died years ago. The son, however, has done very well for himself in America."

XIII

Bricker was dead.

"Which goes to show," said Rodney, "that payment comes in stages."

Bricker's cause of death was an intestinal complaint, per the official report prepared by Governor Norton and sent South by packet Indian to the governor of York Fort. On the authority of mess hall chatter, Jeremiah learned that the letter also included an evaluation of Bricker's character. The man was a layabout, bedridden most days on account of either illness or drink and not fit to serve the company. The governor and other officers had already decided that he would return on the next supply ship before his contract expired.

In the mess hall, Jeremiah stared into the distance. His spruce beer tasted uglier than usual, and he saw Bricker as he was, his square, strong body leading the dogs hitched to a sleigh laden with firewood across the snow. Also, the man himself hitched to a sled, dragging back the meat of a caribou that the Homeguard Cree had killed. Or, hauling at the pulley rope to lift heavy stones for the mason who stood on scaffolding and was mending the Fort wall. Yes, Jeremiah had been on the ramparts that day to help guide the stones and had seen a Native woman arrive with partridges hanging out of a basket that she carried on her back. Bricker's face lit up, and he gave a small wave. The woman looked down, but not before Jeremiah saw a smile spread across her face.

Perhaps the governor had seen that too.

The story was the story, and by all appearances, the governor wrote that story. When would he write Jeremiah's story, the young man wondered, decide his destiny, scratch words on parchment that, in their permanency, would erase the reality of his life? He suddenly felt the urge to go.

If the governor had killed Bricker, Jeremiah thought, he did so at the most opportune moment. Samuel Hearne and a chief named Matonabbee had just arrived at the Fort, and Jeremiah judged that this Matonabbee was an important man as all hands were on deck to put on a feast fit for royalty.

The English officers and Chipewyan chief with his lieutenant and officers had just sat down in the dining room, the scene familiar to Jeremiah, the oak tables end to end with chipped china dishes and glass goblets. The officers and Matonabbee's men chose wine, port, or brandy as their tastes inclined. Jeremiah, yet again in the footmen uniform with a clean white towel over his arm, silver tray in hand, filled the goblets from decanters on the side board.

He was not sure if the insult of this assignment even mattered. He was, after all, not officially an officer and, he admitted, was happy to be in the dining room tonight. This Native Matonabbee was an impressive figure. As Jeremiah poured the chief a Spanish wine, apparently his favorite and kept in stock just for him, he got a closer look at this giant man. He was over six feet tall in a fine caribou suit embroidered at collar and hems with a bright pattern alternating geometric shapes and renditions of animals from these lands. He was, perhaps, the most handsome Indian that Jeremiah had ever seen, and his English was quite good. Jeremiah tried to avert his eyes, but moments later would catch himself ogling yet again.

"Chief Matonabbee and Mr. Hearne," the surgeon began at dinner, "we are much interested to hear of your adventures."

Samuel Hearne, his face gaunt and weatherbeaten, hair sparse as though blown away or lost without enough to eat, responded, "Sadly, gentlemen, I did not reach the copper mine or the Northern Sea."

To Mr. Hearne's right sat the lovely young woman, the governor's daughter, whom they called Mary. Jeremiah positioned himself to the right of the sideboard to catch a better glimpse of this elusive creature whose melodies and fine voice he'd heard through that frustratingly cloudy window but whose face he had never seen.

"What's your excuse this time, Hearne?" muttered George Spurrell, his mouth full of goose meat. "The guide again?"

At this, side glances were shot at the governor to gauge his reaction. As Jeremiah had learned, the governor engaged his own Cree relatives and friends to lead both of Mr. Hearne's failed expeditions.

The governor looked unaffected, as though someone had just told him the sun was high in the sky and whales could be seen out to sea. He took a leisurely sip of his port.

"There were, I must admit, a variety of factors that hampered my success." Mr. Hearne let out a long sigh, that of a man disappointed yet again, and Jeremiah saw Mary take hold of his hand beneath the table.

Her dark skin contrasted with her cream-colored gown, which was embroidered with blue flowers and green leaves. Unlike English gentlewomen, with their lily-white skin, deep red silks, and blue taffetas, Mary's shone against the light fabric. Her dark hair was thick, shiny, and woven in plaits. Jeremiah could see the translator girl, now Mary's lady in waiting, behind her.

"And what say you, man?" boomed Sir George. "What befell you this time?"

"Well, Sir George," said Mr. Hearne, "I admit to losing all hope when my quadrant blew off a rocky outcrop and smashed to pieces—the bubble, sight-vane, and vernier beyond repair. I had left the instrument with the intention to move it to a lower altitude and obtain another latitude to compare with my first. Also, my guide, companions, and I were robbed of our few remaining possessions upon return."

Chief Matonabbee spoke. "As I told Mr. Hearne, the failure of his expedition was the lack of women. Women are essential travel companions in our lands. My wives carry upwards of sixty pounds as well as cook, dress furs, sew clothing and moccasins, haul the meat and wood. They also require very little sustenance."

"With all respect, Governor," said Hearne, looking eagerly at Mr. Norton, who returned Hearne's intense gaze with a blank stare, "I owe my life to Matonabbee and his people. He lent me and my Cree companions winter suits of otter and enough moccasins to last us for the return journey. We would surely have perished from the elements without his aid."

"Well, looks like he'd be," said Spurrell, pointing his fat finger Matonabbee's way, "a good Indian to hire for the next undertaking."

"We have already made promises to engage Chief Keelshies for the next expedition," said the governor.

Matonabbee nodded and said, "I have respect for Chief Keelshies; he is a great hunter and trapper. I would not discourage you from taking that course, if you saw fit. However, I was sent by the preceding governor of this Fort to find the mine and come from there."

"You have seen the mine?" declared the surgeon, and the English officers around the table muttered, impressed.

"Is there a great deal of copper? Did you see the great Northern Sea?" exclaimed the warehouse keeper.

"I did see large pieces of copper and have brought you one." Here, Matonabbee motioned to his lieutenant, who produced a piece of copper ore from a bag at his side. Matonabbee passed the rock to the surgeon and the officers handed it around, each man admiring the piece. When it was finally handed to Jeremiah, he guessed it weighed upwards of five pounds.

"As to the Northern Sea, I do not know." Matonabbee motioned to Mr. Hearne. "My friend and I have engaged in many discussions in which we both have learned a great deal from the other's wisdom and trade. He uses the horizon, stars, and his gadgets to calculate distances, and yes, there is what resembles a great sea at the mouth of what has been called the Coppermine River. Running along this river, pieces of copper can be found."

Chief Matonabbee now had the rapt attention of all the officers, whose eyes shone like golden guineas. They began to ask if had he seen a metal more like silver or gold in those parts. Matonabbee apologized. He had not.

"We did find it peculiar, Chief," began the surgeon, "that your women wear copper jewelry. Keelshies said your people do not wear copper adornment and disowned the very copper necklace his own wife wore as belonging to this girl." The surgeon gestured toward Shenan.

The translator girl, Jeremiah saw, watched the proceedings keenly from behind her mistress, with that sparkle in her eye that Jeremiah found intelligent and a little menacing.

George Spurrell then chimed in, "Chief, the squaw speaks English and is attending Lady Mary. Claims she is the descendant of some family of translators. Of course, none of us believes it."

"That is most interesting," said Chief Matonabbee and nodded at the girl, who did not appear to notice as she was staring Spurrell down with her dark, ominous eyes.

Sir George burst out, "You can point that gaze somewhere else, you little witch."

The room quieted for a moment, then the surgeon said hastily, "We were inquiring into the difference between your people and Keelshies's, that though of the same tribe he disdains the copper decoration."

Here Matonabbee nodded as though considering this, then conferred with his lieutenant and other officers around the table. "My apologies. I wanted to be sure of my recollection. There is a woman that travels with Chief Keelshies, though we believe she is no longer with him. Her name is Waawaatee. She is a healer and keeper of rituals amongst our people. Keelshies believes this woman killed his mother through a copper bracelet."

At this, a great clatter was heard and all eyes turned to the slave-now-lady-in-waiting who had dropped a pewter pitcher. She did not seem to register that all eyes were upon her, and she stared into the distance with a stunned expression.

"Honestly, Governor," yelled Spurrell, "the squaw you've taken on is touched!"

His booming voice appeared to jar the girl, and after shooting Spurrell another piercing glare, she made a few hasty apologies. Mary and Samuel Hearne rose from their chairs and began to help the girl pick up the pitcher and clean the mess.

Matonabbee was nonplussed and continued as though there had been no disturbance. "As you gentlemen know, the Esquimaux are our enemies. Many years ago, our people and the Esquimaux were at war and Keelshies's father took a copper bracelet off a dead Esquimaux girl. He gave the bracelet to Waawaatee, not his wife . . ." Matonabbee again conferred with his men, and one spoke at length, at which all began to nod.

"Yes, the story goes that Waawaatee was unwilling to accept the bracelet and left it in the wife's tent. The wife, Keelshies's mother, thought this was a gift from her husband and wore the bracelet. She was dead three days following. Keelshies has believed since that Waawaatee cursed the jewelry, as the sorceress is said to have some powers with the copper metal."

The officers around the table seemed to puzzle this over when finally Spurrell said, "Sounds like a bunch of malarkey to me. Hearne," he yelled down the table, "have you heard of this, the witch, magic powers, something with the copper?"

"Excuse me?" Hearne, who was just resuming his seat after assisting Mary's maid, looked confused.

At this, Matonabbee and his men rose. Governor Norton and the officers quickly got to their feet.

"Our sincerest apologies, Chief," the surgeon began to sputter, indicating in the direction of Sir George. Jeremiah also thought that Matonabbee's abrupt exit was worrisome, and the Chief was perhaps offended by the fat little man. Spurrell was most troublesome tonight, and Jeremiah began to wonder if he was starting to lose his mind. The culprit sat unaware, sucking the marrow noisily out of a goose bone.

Moses Norton asked, "Are you departing for the evening, Chief?"

"Yes, the journey has been long, and we traveled hard today since before the sun rose." Matonabbee continued, his voice sincere, "Please, gentlemen, have no trouble on our part. The dinner was excellent, and we thank you for your generosity." At this, Matonabbee, with his officers trailing behind, walked about the table, shaking every man's hand including Spurrell's, whose paw was covered in goose fat. Matonabbee shook it without blinking an eye.

"Governor," Samuel Hearne said, standing up quickly and bowing his head, "may Matonabbee and I have an audience tomorrow? As we discussed, I loath to leave again, so soon." He looked at Mary. "But I am eager to cover miles while the snow is still good for the sleds and dogs."

"Yes, my office hours are at the usual time." Governor Norton then asked his servant to fetch a lantern and said, "I will escort the chief back to camp." At this, Mary also stood. She bowed to Mr. Hearne, and Jeremiah could see their hands brush and fingers linger.

Mary and her lady-in-waiting exited first then were followed by the governor, who led out Matonabbee and his men. Hearne then made his excuses, begged forgiveness for his early departure, and was also gone.

With the room so vacated, the surgeon turned to Spurrell and said, "Really, George, you are most insolent with the Natives."

"Ah," Spurrell said, pushing back his chair, his large paunch now enormous after the feast and flush with the table. "Did you hear the man? A copper witch, curses, and dead mothers?" He laughed heartily. "Such stories don't exist in the Bible, that I'm sure of."

"Never mind, Hearne," said the warehouse keeper, waving dismissively at Spurrell and looking foul. "Spurrell jests at the expense of our honored guest when he believes myths himself like the one concerning James Knight."

The room quieted, and Jeremiah felt uneasy. The legend of James Knight was a known sore spot around this table; the warehouse keeper believed Governor Knight, who had ruled this Bay in the early 1700s, had died by starvation along with his crew on Marble Island. Spurrell believed the Esquimaux massacred Knight and his crew. And though Jeremiah could not fathom why both men cared so much, it was a known source of tension between them. Why the warehouse keeper would choose this moment to raise the subject, when Sir George was in such a state, was beyond Jeremiah's comprehension.

"I do say, and I do say again, by the word of many gentlemen," Spurrell began in a voice of strained calm, which Jeremiah felt was a bad sign, "James Knight during his search for the Northwest Passage, to the great glory of England and our King, was murdered by the Esquimaux. Of this, there can be no doubt, that we would not sit here today awaiting Samuel Hearne to find the Northwest Passage, as James Knight would have found it sixty years ago if not for the treachery of those savages."

"Although this was long the accepted story, Sir George, with all due respect—" The surgeon tried to insert himself; Jeremiah was sure to try and ward off an escalation.

But Sir George interrupted, his face red as a tomato about to burst. "Yes, a tale that some Esquimaux savage would have you believe!"

"I don't believe that the Esquimaux Elder from whom we have this information would have fabricated such a tale. As well, when their remains were found, there were no signs of struggle, only starvation. This should not even be under discussion." The warehouse keeper spoke in a tone that pretended calm but hinted a storm.

"You are to tell me," Sir George spoke measured and tight, "that you truly believe this Elder. His story that Knight's last surviving men"—his voice took on a mocking tone, his portly body shaking back and forth—"stood on a hilltop, clutching one another, signaling to a ship on the horizon then collapsed in grief, just for one to die and the other to die digging that other's grave. Honestly, men! Sounds like a play put on at the theater. I say the savage should be writing for the queen. I'll tell you, James Knight the old badger allowed the Esquimaux on the island and trusted them. One day later, the Esquimaux had all manner of treasures and a feast of roasted flesh."

This back and forth on James Knight between Spurrell and the warehouse keeper was not unfamiliar to the men around this table. They had heard this argument more times than they cared to count, though never with emotions this high.

"Calm yourselves, gentlemen," said the surgeon.

"Believe what you want, Spurrell," spat the warehouse keeper, "since you sit here on your fat arse all day and have not once ventured to trade with the Esquimaux and don't know their ways. They are civil and industrious, not a dawdler and loaf like you."

"You blackguard!" bellowed Sir George. "I've seen more honest men than you hung at Tyburn. We are all wise to your stash of furs at Button Bay."

"That's none of your concern!" shouted the warehouse keeper. "You speak of Tyburn when your own treasonous cousin was carted up Holburn Hill to the gallows!"

This was news to Jeremiah, that George had a cousin who had been hanged.

"That's it," cried Sir George, and he struggled his voluminous self over the table, glass goblet shattering on the floor and shards of porcelain skittering into corners. The warehouse keeper also stood, and the two began to grapple. The surgeon threw his chair back and tried to shimmy under the table but struggled to get past one of the legs.

Just then, John America caught Jeremiah's eye. The boy was standing beside the double doors that led out of the hall. He darted between red-faced gentlemen, the accomptant entangled with the steward, the surgeon, in his pacific attempts, knocked down by a glancing blow, long simmering tensions at long last boiling over.

John America bent down and whispered, "The men in the mess hall, they are most unruly though in better spirits than," he said, looking around, "these men. Yet, they are pounding the tables and chanting 'Broach it, broach it.' The men from the Orkneys, they have drug up a hogshead of brandy from the cellar—without Father's permission."

"The governor has gone to take Matonabbee back to camp. You must go fetch him," Jeremiah shouted over the scuffle and yells of the fighting gentlemen.

John America shook his head. "He did not go. He sent another man and . . ." John America paused, then he said in a rush, "he went to his rooms. He's in there with his friends and women, and the door is locked."

Even Jeremiah knew not to disturb the governor when he was so engaged.

"Nothing can be done," said Jeremiah. "Those that would stop it—" He was interrupted by another clang of metal and shattering of glass as serving trays fell and goblets crashed to the ground.

Jeremiah then saw the face of George Spurrell contort and his entire body go rigid. His eyes bulged and stared fixedly at the wall. He collapsed to the ground.

"He's seizing," yelled the surgeon, pushing back the warehouse keeper and turning Spurrell on his side as the man shook uncontrollably with unseeing eyes. "George, George!" yelled the surgeon into the man's face. "Can you hear me?"

"He's in the midst of an apoplectic fit," said the surgeon. "Fetch men from the mess hall to help carry him." Jeremiah sprang, sprinting outside to the mess hall where he could hear the fiddle from across the courtyard. The men in the hall had broached the hogshead of brandy, the fiddle strummed a lively tune, and the men were dancing as the Orkney men do, tapping feet and kicking their legs in the air. A few were standing on tables, arms thrown over their neighbors' shoulders and stomping their feet. Jeremiah rushed to the tailor, ruddy in the face but alert, and then grabbed Rodney. They rushed back to the dining room, where the tailor stopped short in the doorway to see fine china and glass strewn across the floor. Chairs were overturned, with officers lying on the floor next to their opposition, tired, bleeding, and panting. The fighting appeared at a halt. The three rushed to Sir George, grabbed him beneath the arms and legs, and followed the surgeon to the infirmary.

XIV

Shenan heard Mary and Samuel Hearne as she came down the passageway with a load of wood. She set it down gingerly and worked her way behind the door. She could hear the faint sound of someone crying.

Hearne said gently, "Mary, your father will not give us his permission until I distinguish myself and bring this to completion. The sea route to the Orient, the Northwest Passage, the copper mine that the Natives have reported for decades, I don't know if they even exist. The closer I get, the more I doubt it. But I am consumed with the possibility and by my own failures. As well, I know if I can make it, your father will rise in the company's esteem as the man who sent me. Only then will he be pleased with me, and only then will he consent to us."

"I cry because I am so happy to see you though I cannot lie—I do not want to part so soon," Mary said.

"Mary." The man's voice was intense and sounded sincere. "You are my life and heart. If I can't marry you, it would be like death to me. I would be incomplete."

"I worry that you won't return." Mary's voice was strained.

There was a pause. Shenan had to admit, Samuel Hearne sounded honest in his intentions, and these two were clearly fond of one another.

"I have almost died. I would have died, but God was with me when he sent Matonabbee. He is like no other Native I have ever met.

Many men follow him, and when the caribou are plentiful he has a camp upwards of two hundred. From his descriptions, I believe he has seen the Northern Sea, and with his knowledge and influence I may finally succeed."

"He was most gracious at dinner," Mary concurred.

"The only part of his character that I find troubling . . ." Hearne paused. "Dare I say, he is a jealous man who does not tolerate insolence from his wives. He did beat one wife, and I know not if she survived. I fear she did not. But it appears to be the way in these lands. Your own father—"

Hearne stopped talking, and Shenan wondered if Mary stayed him with her hand. Mary, as a rule, did not discuss or listen to any talk that involved the governor and his women.

There was a pause, and then Hearne said in a burst, as though he could not contain himself, "Don't you understand, Mary? These women, they are his crown, his scepter, his ermine gown. They are his trappings of power. He is suspected, known, to have killed men . . ."

He drifted off, and Shenan heard him sigh as though defeated.

Shenan could not hear the fire crackle and became impatient as it needed tending. Besides, Mary was tardy for her evening visit to the governor's rooms.

"I'm sorry," said Hearne. He sounded resigned, like one fatigued who lost a battle. "All that matters, Mary, is our lives will be very different. I know your father wants you in England, but, Mary, I know that is not best for you. Your father did not grow up in England. The fine ladies there will invite you once for tea as a curiosity to see your skin and hear you talk, but they will not accept you into their circles. If we have children, God willing, their opportunities will be here. I see us in the evenings by the fire, you sewing or reading, and myself, drawing and writing. I have so many things to write about this place. I love you."

"I love you," Mary answered.

Shenan heard kissing. She wondered if Mr. Hearne knew it was troublesome to relight a fire and much less work just to keep it going.

She then heard footsteps in the passageway and quickly stepped out before Governor Norton rounded the corner. His stride was bent and determined toward Mary's room, as Shenan suspected might happen, the governor concerned because his daughter was late for her nightly visit.

"Hello, Governor." Shenan bowed her head, eyes to the ground. The rustlings in Mary's room came to a stop.

"Why do you stand there, girl, in the shadows?" The governor, annoyed, did not want an answer. He was already expecting Shenan to step aside so he could enter Mary's room.

"I dropped a pin just there, as Mary sent me to fetch a few. She is with the tailor. Her bodice came undone and a seam of the back pleating . . ." She drifted off. She sensed the governor's impatience, never interested in such details.

The governor nodded and his eyes looked, as they usually did when he came to Mary's room, troubled and stormy. "Tell Mary to come for her visit when she has finished."

"Yes, sir, I will." To her relief, the governor turned on his heel and left as he came.

Shenandoah followed right behind to keep up the ruse that she was on her way to the tailor's rooms and to give Mr. Hearne the opportunity to make a hasty escape.

XV

The next morning, the Fort was so still that it reminded Shenan of the morning after a village was raided or a treaty negotiated, the smoke and wind moving more than the drunk or dead. Only a few men rose for breakfast while the majority were ill and kept to bed. The few that got up huddled outside the kitchens and did not take their meal in the mess hall. Shenan was then asked to clean both the dining room and mess hall, and she understood.

Apparently, after Shenan and Mary left the dining room the previous night, a fight had broken out and Sir George suffered some sort of fit. She had spent all morning cleaning up broken pieces of porcelain plates and shards of glass. Then, she had moved on to the mess hall, scrubbing corners that reeked of urine, stones and cracks covered in vomit, and the tabletops wore more brandy, she thought, than could possibly have made it inside the men.

Shenan then moved on to the governor's rooms, which she cleaned daily in the late afternoon before dressing Mary. His rooms at this time looked very different than when she and Mary would retire for the night. After she and Mary left, the bacchanal must begin. Empty bottles and cups everywhere, sticky dried liquid on every surface, clothing both male and female strewn across chairs and around the bed. *Oh,* Shenan thought, rubbing her temples, *the bed*. Always torn to pieces and had to be taken down completely every afternoon and remade.

Shenan tried to ignore the squawking of the governor's infernal parrot. Its bright feathers were so out of place in the grey and dark interior that Shenan often had to blink and adjust her eyes. He either made the walls red and yellow or his brightness somehow just accentuated the grey.

"Let us be friends, Bricker, a toast." This was the parrot's new phrase today, on repeat. Also, "Poor fellow, poor fellow, poor fellow," the parrot would say and then cackle, his caw like a hysterical child with a hint of mania that could almost be confused with glee. She had heard this same deranged laugh many a time hidden behind Mary's door during the governor's long delusional monologues.

The next day, the officers hung their heads, though only slightly, as they were gentlemen possessed of an immutable sense of greatness.

Jeremiah witnessed a few encounters and awkward conversations between men that just the night before had grappled at each other like schoolboys in the yard.

These conversations were marked by mumblings such as "Well, that was something," and "I did my part," and "I certainly held my own." The officers, with an equal show of pride and contrition, were comrades again, though thrashing and flailing at each other only hours earlier.

Jeremiah saw the warehouse keeper shake the hand of the steward with a "drink on it tonight and all forgotten."

Also, "I do hope Sir George will be on the mend soon," as Spurrell remained in the infirmary and had been attended all night by the surgeon.

The day went for the most part as any other day, and Jeremiah found himself where he always ended up, on second night watch. He headed first to the governor's window and was pleasantly regaled with a concert. Mary's sweet alto mingled with a baritone, which Jeremiah could only imagine belonged to her lover, Samuel Hearne.

The night was shaping up to be quiet in terms of activity at the gate and profits for Rodney. It was especially cold. Jeremiah found these long, lonely nights to be interminable and dreary. The crack of shifting ice pierced the air, followed by silence. The solitude of these unanswered sounds made Jeremiah's thoughts reverberate. The expansive night sky pushed on his chest like a weight while the dark sea opened wide, and he envisioned the sky crushing him while the sea swallowed him whole.

When he returned to their small fire, Rodney produced a satchel from his pocket. It was the type of bag that the Natives carried and contained objects important to them—a tuft of hair from a loved one, prized eagle or hawk feathers, a woodpecker's red forehead, sometimes medicines or objects used in rituals. He had learned a few things, spending time at Segenam's camp. The center of this bag had a triangular design of red, purple, and white porcupine quills that ran straight and smooth through the bag's center. Those blue beads that had caused all the trouble adorned the bottom edge.

"Where did you get that, Rodney?" Jeremiah hissed, his eyes drawn immediately to the beads, the same he had given away to the old woman and slave while keeping the accounts.

"On my way back from Segenam's yesterday, that old woman was waiting for me. She wants me to give it to Mary's slave or lady in waiting, whatever she is. Though at first, I thought to keep it for myself. Something to show my kids, my grandchildren, something for the wife." He waved his hand as though to dispel the notion. "Then I thought, *I'll give it to the boy, as something to remember me by*. Anyway, I had scads of these gee gaws."

He extended the bag to Jeremiah, who shrank away. "I'm not taking that! I'm already implicated in the theft of those beads! Why not just give it to the girl?"

Rodney scoffed. "Son, if I can hide piles of furs and trade goods, you think you can't hide a bag?" He looked disgusted and brought it back toward himself. "Fine, I'll keep it then."

"You should give it to the girl, Rodney." Jeremiah heard his own voice, low and fearful. "That woman, even on the word of Chief Matonabbee, is a known sorceress. With my own eyes I saw her curse Chief Keelshies, who was trembling like a leaf."

Rodney looked at him as if he had two heads and had gone out of his mind. "Now, that is something I didn't think I'd hear. An Englishman believing the Native's superstitions. That is something."

Jeremiah clammed up and felt foolish for what he said. He did believe it. He believed it with all his heart and was suddenly ashamed that he did.

He stuck his hand out. "Give me the damned bag." Rodney rolled his eyes and slapped it into Jeremiah's outstretched palm with a slap. "At least I can give it to the rightful owner."

"Whatever you say, son. I thought it might be a nice trinket for you but wouldn't want the Native Spirits to get you." Rodney mocked Jeremiah, waving his fingers in the air and drawing out a low noise, which was Rodney's poor imitation of a ghost or evil being.

Jeremiah sat in the chair, rose again, then paced about the fire in irritation and agitation. He finally let out a "Damn it all," and stalked away, preferring the company of lonely winds that howled and the governor's debauched rooms to this old codger.

XVI

Before Samuel Hearne and Matonabbee's departure, Mary tended Sir George every other night, alternating with other employees who volunteered so that the surgeon could rest. Hearne had departed three days hence, and Mary had been with Sir George every night since.

At times, Shenandoah was summoned to prop the man upright as Mary spooned broth or porridge into his mouth. It trickled down his chin, and Mary gently wiped it away. Sir George stared at Mary with adoring eyes and squeezed tight in his contracted hand a cross that John America had whittled for him.

If Shenan had been left in charge, she would have shoved a biscuit down this throat to put him out of his misery and because she didn't like the man.

During one such night, when Shenan sat alone in Mary's room on the rug, she saw a shadow fall over the light that spilled out of the doorway. A soft tap sounded on the door, and the apprentice Jeremiah entered.

His face was flushed, and his eyes darted around the room. He produced Waawaatee's satchel. Those blue beads, the ones Shenan knew had caused quite a fuss, looked as blue as a robin's egg when reflected in the light of the fire.

"I've been asked to deliver . . . this," the young man stammered. "A gift from the old lady."

Shenan raised her eyebrows and said, "No one gifts their god bag, as you'd call it." She did not feel obligated to explain to this young man, who probably wouldn't understand anyway, that these bundles were sacred. The transfer of a sacred bundle from one individual to another was preceded by years of apprenticeship and training. The moment of passage was an event of profound importance and the occasion of a great ceremony.

Waawaatee had been sending this bag through the fall and winter with John America to be replenished. The surgeon supplied Waawaatee with a few simple medicines such as sulphur, bark, liquorice, camphorated spirit, white ointment, and basilicon. Shenan was quite certain that Waawaatee used these to supplement her own medicines and make them more palatable to the Homeguard Cree.

As Shenan, Mary, and John America sat together before the fire as fall turned into winter, Shenan had told the story of her time with the Chipewyans. Inevitably, Waawaatee's role emerged as her protector and mother.

Mary, because her heart and kindness were as expansive as the sky and as vast as the tundra, gifted Waawaatee a red leather trunk that contained these medicines. This trunk was traditionally given to the prominent wife of a chief or a healer within a trading party.

The true value of the red leather trunk, John America said, was protection. It signaled to the Cree relatives of Mary, John America, and Governor Norton that Waawaatee possessed some connection to the Fort. Before, she was a stranger, unknown and expendable, but now she was an important and connected person. John America said that Waawaatee displayed her trunk for all to see, atop a stump in the corner of her tree root hut.

The surgeon had been the unlikely source for Waawaatee's refills. He would usher John America and Shenan into an empty infirmary, turn the lock quietly, and the three would listen awhile for any sounds in the hall. John America would produce the sacred bundle only once the three were certain that no one was outside the door. The surgeon would take the little bags and containers from Waawaatee's satchel then head to his spice box and cupboard and fill them with powders and ointments. The man appreciated a skilled healer outside the walls of the Fort.

"Most winters, I have one to two Natives in the infirmary at all times," he told them, adding that they were typically brought on sleds by relatives who were sick themselves. "Problem is, children, the London Committee doesn't approve. They imagine these sick Natives eat up the entire cellar, but in reality they are too ill to take much but thin porridge and they die on my hands as well. I am of the opinion that they fare poorly within the close walls of the Fort, but don't we all."

The bag would go back to John America, who would abscond it within his own bundle to deliver on his next trip home. John America, however, had not been home in weeks, as Matonabbee and his men had eaten dinner every night in the dining room and breakfast every morning. Shenan had seen John America and that young apprentice Jeremiah running dishes back and forth from the kitchens since the chief's arrival.

With Matonabbee's and Hearne's departures, Shenan imagined that John America would not be long in returning home. The boy, however, had not the opportunity, what with the warehouse to be put back in order, the unbroken dishes to be gone through and made into a proper set, and the Christmas holiday nigh, which brought its own special distribution of provisions. John America was at the beck and call of the steward, who was taking inventory of the foodstuffs to determine what could be spared for the Christmas holiday.

Shenan rose from the rug and said, "Thank you," giving Jeremiah a small smile, which seemed to encourage the nervous young man. He had, in all fairness, sought her out to deliver the bag, and she should show him a little kindness. If she were asked to deliver an English item to someone of no importance to her, she might hide or sell the thing.

At this moment, another person cast a shadow over the light that spilled into the hallway. Jeremiah was holding out the bag, Shenan was reaching for it, and they both looked toward the door and locked eyes with Governor Norton. He stared at them, and they stared back too stunned to move. The bag fell from Jeremiah's hand to the floor.

Later, when Shenan replayed the moment in her mind, she was struck by the governor's expression. He was not angry or displeased, perhaps not joyous, but most definitely satisfied. He had finally caught someone, in the flesh, in the act, doing what he always knew went on within these walls.

Jeremiah showed up for second night watch, and instead of Rodney, his two friends were back. He had since learned their names, James Down and James Calbant. As one looked a few years older than the other and they were always together, the men had acquired the nicknames Brother James and Baby James. They sat in the chairs next to the stone ring and were holding an unsanctioned bottle that Jeremiah had seen Rodney trade, just a few nights before, to let an officer's woman in the door.

They gave him a dismissive nod, and Jeremiah stood while the other two sat. The mood was desultory without Rodney's presence and incessant chatter.

Jeremiah kicked a clump of ice and said, "What I can't understand is who told the governor. How could he have known that I would be delivering that bag?"

The mess hall was alight with the news that Jeremiah had been caught passing the missing beads to the slave girl. The men were relieved that the culprit had been found and their bonus, silver plate or equivalent token of gratitude, was no longer threatened.

The men had more theories than fingers, John America told Jeremiah. One, the apprentice stole the beads and gave them to the slave girl, who, in all likelihood, was his bedmate. Or, Jeremiah stole them for no other reason than they were shiny, but fearing the sorceress in the woods he sent them to her for protection from her curses and spells. Jeremiah could hear Rodney behind that one. The most outlandish: Jeremiah was half-Chipewyan himself, smuggled to

England as an infant, and the sorceress was his grandmother. Per John America's telling, however, Jeremiah's fair skin and the red tint to his hair kept this one mere fancy and just amusing to repeat.

Brother James stretched back and answered Jeremiah's question. "Oh bleeding heart, it was Rodney. He informed on you."

"Rodney?" Jeremiah was incredulous. "That's absurd!"

"Oh, it was, apprentice," said Baby James. "And what's more, he told us to tell you."

"Why in God's name would Rodney . . ." He drifted off. His mentor, his teacher, his nemesis most every night, dare he call him a friend? Even the notion was ridiculous.

Baby said, "Oh, some rubbish about he's seen it a dozen times. The young ones, the governor takes against them, writes a poor character, they can't find another position, never amount to anything in this place, he went on and on."

"You know, old Rodney speaks some sense. The governor has no liking for you," said Brother. "And look what happened to Bricker—one of the hardest working men in this place now cast as some drunken loafer."

"He says you need to go," said Baby. "If he'd had learning and such as you when he was a boy, he'd have been off to Montreal by now."

Jeremiah balked. "Rodney expects me to set out in the dead of winter? I'll starve, freeze to death for sure!"

The two acted as if they didn't hear him, and Baby said, "Oh yes, he says if you make it to Montreal he has a Scottish cousin. Last name is McTavish. First name is probably Douglas or some such."

"The first name was not Douglas. Maybe it was Angus," said Brother.

"Duncan, John, who knows," said Baby, now peevish. "May have been Simon."

"We don't remember, but he lives in Montreal and take your time as your letter of introduction won't arrive for two years. He's sending it on the next supply ship."

"Maybe three. He's not sending it by packet Indian or anything. That would cost a fortune," chimed in Brother.

As usual, the night felt like a dream, even more so tonight with Rodney absent and the absurd notion that Jeremiah was going to run. However, was it absurd? He had thought before about leaving. He could go to Segenam's camp, spend a few days, weeks, the rest of the winter. His prospects and reputation were already ruined, and he had nothing to lose. Years ago, a young apprentice that Jeremiah had heard of, by the name of Anthony Henday, did much the same and when he returned years later after exploring the hinterlands, he was promoted and favored by the company.

"Rodney leave me any of that?" Jeremiah asked, motioning to the bottle.

Brother and Baby chuckled. "Should've secured your own, big man. We'll give you one drink before you go."

Jeremiah took his drink and handed it back. "I guess I'll just walk out then," he said, almost daring them. Was this really happening, and did he have any other choice? Stay here and be sent back on the next supply ship, perhaps lose all his wages, go home a failure. Remain on second night watch with Rodney, who he was quite certain had not informed on him. But who else knew he would be delivering the satchel to the slave girl at that moment?

Suddenly, he wanted to go. He was tired of this place, the men either surly and working or drunk and teasing. Each night, he was closer to frostbite and losing his toes. He wanted to get lost awhile in that expansive tundra and land of sticks beyond. He had a place he could stay for a while, and maybe he would come back, master of languages, hunter and trapper extraordinaire, a trail of Natives behind him with canoes piled high with furs.

"Good luck. Get your tools and such, boy. And Rodney left you a gun where he stashes his things."

Jeremiah went to his room and packed his meager possessions—the blanket with the stripes, the tools he had never used, his writing box with a few pieces of parchment, and the locket that contained his sister's hair. He was already wearing every article of clothing that he owned as he did every night.

He returned to the gate thinking that someone would spring out—the carpenter, the armourer, one of the jesters from the mess hall. Rodney would emerge, the man of the hour, and they would all have a good laugh. In the end, it would be a prank, to break up and enliven this long and dreary season.

But when he got back, Brother and Baby sat much as they did before and the air held the same dull thrum.

Well then, he would go. He'd take on their challenge. Maybe he'd stay a few days then come back.

"Well, get on with it. Let me out," said Jeremiah.

They looked at him skeptically. "You think we're letting you out the door? The governor has spies all over this place."

"How else do you expect me to get out of a stone fortress?" Jeremiah asked incredulously.

"Apprentice named Henday, years ago, he jumped the wall. You can manage it, you've got a young back," said Baby.

The two went back to their mutterings, and Jeremiah stood staring at them. He stalked off toward the walls, no plan in mind except to wander the interior, stare across the silver snow, and curse this place.

Once outside, with no way back in until morning, Jeremiah hesitated. It was one thing to show up at Segenam's during the day laden with gifts. It was another to come emptyhanded in the middle of the night. He looked behind the pile, to find a gun, bag of shot, and two powder horns. Everything else was gone.

He couldn't believe it. It really had been Rodney. Was this because he knew too much about Rodney's private trading operation?

"Rodney." Jeremiah spat the name as though he wanted it out

of his mouth, but it lingered there, leaving a foul taste. Rodney, who was forever proclaiming himself old, decrepit, and frail. Who would push the furs to the back of his cave now? Honestly, the bastard could probably have done it himself all along.

He could give Segenam the gun, but was he to lounge about, lie with the man's daughter, make a nuisance of himself, no way to hunt or fend for himself?

He heard a thud and saw a bundle hit the ground, then, a moment later, he heard a softer thud. He and the translator girl locked eyes as she landed. She must have thrown her bundle over the ramparts then squeezed through the embrasure past the cannon, just as he did.

She was escaping too, which made sense. He'd be sent back to England, fined or wages gone. She might be sent to her death, shoved out the gates without enough clothing to make it even one hundred feet. She threw her bundle onto her back, securing it, and eyed him warily.

Weren't they though, he thought, in this together? He could see how, if he left with her, it would be difficult to protest his innocence down the road. But the air was bitter, his feet already felt like blocks of ice, and he could hear the waves of that uncrossable sea at his back. There had always been a strength to this girl, he realized. She emanated a toughness that in this moment he needed.

Without really thinking, he approached and grabbed her hand. In return, she shot him a look that would burn down a house, and he dropped it.

※※※※※※※※※※※※※※※※※※※※※※

Shenan knew as she squared off against this fool outside the walls of the Fort that she was a very different girl than two years before. Two years ago, when Uncle Andrew abandoned her, she didn't understand that the only person who valued her life, was her. Now this was a fact as clear as the sharp cold air, and the fixed and frozen stars that suspended sparkling above her. If she awoke tomorrow to the taunting eyes of two

French voyageurs, she would smile and demur then gut them both at the first opportunity. She would hold no man's hand.

This young man could come, harmless by appearance, but with one wrong step she'd leave his bowels strewn on the snow for the wolves and crows. And that look would be the last and only warning that he would get. This was her moment to find her way home or maybe just to find her way.

She thought of Mary's eyes, which reminded her of stones on a lakebed that one could only see when the water was so clear that the sun reached the bottom. Love was for some people, but it wasn't for her. Love was buried in graves or in the sky or deep in the sea. She didn't really know where it had gone. She knew it still lived in some people, like Samuel and Mary, but it wouldn't live in her, again.

As the two started off across the snow, the silent petty dancers, those Northern Lights, tonight of green pink and blue, reflected and lit the way.

The lone figures on the limitless stretch weren't sure, in this harsh, inhospitable, and beautiful barren world, if the lights danced because they'd live or danced because they'd die.

AUTHOR'S NOTE

Characters in this novella are based upon people who graced Prince of Wales Fort in 1770, the ruins of which are located across the river from present-day Churchill, Manitoba. Richard Glover (1982), in his article "Moses Norton (ca. late 1720s–1773)," writes that Norton was apprenticed to Captain George Spurrell in 1744. The captain commanded a supply ship that traveled each season from England to the shores of Hudson's Bay. Moses Norton then graduated from apprentice to employee in 1753. Glover states, "The Company engaged [Moses Norton], in 1753, as the Mate of their sloop *Churchill* at the Bay" (p.440). He was appointed chief factor of Prince of Wales Fort in 1762 and held that position until his death in 1773.

In his will, Moses Norton names an Englishwoman, Susan, as his mother, and a biography of the man provided by biography.ca states, "It is possible that Moses was born of an illicit union when his father was on furlough in England in the 1730s." However, the same biography states, "It was not until 1794 that official permission was given for mixed-blood boys to be employed in the company's service," and this may have motivated Moses Norton to misrepresent his origins. One piece of evidence that supports Mr. Norton's Cree ancestry comes from Samuel Hearne. Hearne partially blames the failure of his first two expeditions in search of the Northwest Passage and copper mine on his Cree guides and companions. Hearne declines these escorts for the third expedition, and he writes, in *A Journey from Prince of Wales Fort in Hudson's Bay,* "[Moses Norton] wanted to force some of the home-guard Indians (who were his own relations) into our company . . . I absolutely refused them" (Hearne, 1795, p.39).

The following paragraphs from the same book, *A Journey,* by Hearne, was my jumping-off point in the development of Moses Norton's character:

> Mr. Norton was an Indian; he was born at Prince of Wales's Fort, but had been in England nine years, and considering the small sum which was expended in his education, had made some progress in literature. At his return to Hudson's Bay he entered into all the abominable vices of his countrymen. He kept for his own use five or six of the finest Indian girls which he could select; and notwithstanding his own uncommon propensity to the fair sex, took every means in his power to prevent any European from having intercourse with the women of the country; for which purpose he proceeded to the most ridiculous length. To his own friends and country he was so partial, that he set more value on, and shewed more respect to one of their favourite dogs, than he ever did to his first officer. Among his miserable and ignorant countrymen he passed for a proficient physic, and always kept a box of poison, to administer to those who refused him their wives or daughters.
>
> With all these bad qualities, no man took more pains to inculcate virtue, morality, and continence on others; always painting, in the most odious colours, the jealous and revengeful disposition of the Indians, when any attempt was made to violate the chastity of their wives or daughters. Lectures of this kind from a man of established virtue might have had some effect; but when they came from one who was known

to live in open defiance of every law, human and divine, they were always heard with indignation, and considered as the hypocritical cant of a selfish debauchee, who wished to engross every woman in the country to himself.

His apartments were not only convenient but elegant, and always crowded with his favourite Indians: at night he locked the doors, and put the keys under his pillow; so that in the morning his dining-room was generally, for the want of necessary conveniences, worse than a hog-stye. As he advanced in his years his jealousy increased, and he actually poisoned two of his women because he thought them partial to other objects more suitable to their ages. He was a most notorious smuggler; but though he put many thousands in the pockets of the Captains, he seldom put a shilling into his own.

An inflammation in his bowels occasioned his death on the 29th of December 1773; and though he died in the most excruciating pain, he retained his jealousy to the last; for a few minutes before he expired, happening to see an officer laying hold of the hand of one of his women who was standing by the fire, he bellowed out, in as loud a voice as his situation would admit, 'God d----n you for a b----h, if I live I'll knock out your brains.' A few minutes after making this elegant apostrophe, he expired in the greatest agonies that can possibly be conceived.

This I declare to be the real character and manner of life of the late Mr. Moses Norton. (Hearne, 1795, pp. 39–40).

This lengthy footnote in Hearne's work is presumed to have been written by the author, whose relationship with Governor Norton was reported to have deteriorated over the course of Hearne's three voyages. The piano and parrot in Moses Norton's rooms are noted in the aforementioned biography.ca: "He imported books, pictures, and an organ from England, and even kept a pet parrot." I have not had access to the Hudson's Bay Company Archives in Winnipeg, Manitoba, while writing this book and am not sure if the information regarding the instrument and parrot is in the archives or was an anecdote passed down through time.

Mary Norton was the daughter of Moses Norton, and the lone contemporary reference to Mary that I have found is again contained within the long and revelatory footnotes of *A Journey*, by Hearne. Of Mary, he writes:

> Mary, the daughter of Moses Norton, many years Chief of Prince of Wale's Fort, in Hudson's Bay, though born and brought up in a country of all others the least favorable to virtue and virtuous principles, possessed them, and every other good and amiable quality, in a most eminent degree.
>
> Without the assistance of religion, and with no education but what she received among the dissolute natives of her country, she would have shone with superior lustre in any other country: for, if an engaging person, gentle manners, an easy freedom, arising from consciousness of innocence, an amiable modesty, and an unrivalled delicacy of sentiment, are graces and virtues which render a woman lovely, none ever had greater pretensions to general esteem and regard: while her benevolence, humanity, and scrupulous adherence to truth and honesty, would have done honour to the most enlightened and devout Christian.
>
> Dutiful, obedient and affectionate to her parents; steady and faithful to friends; grateful and humble to her benefactors; easily forgiving and forgetting injuries; careful not to offend any, and courteous and kind to all; she was, nevertheless, suffered to perish by the rigours of cold and hunger, amidst her own relations . . ." (Hearne, 1795, pp. 81–82).

This footnote is again presumed to have been written by Samuel Hearne, with whom, it is reported, Mary enjoyed a happy marriage that bore no children. Mary died in 1782.

Samuel Hearne was the first European to reach the Coronation Gulf and his work, *A Journey,* is considered a valuable record of early colonial discovery and an important ethnological document. Hearne makes a brief appearance in the last third of this novella; indeed, he returns from his second failed voyage on November 25, 1770, and departs with Matonabbee on December 7. Their time at the Fort was a few weeks. My depiction of Hearne arises from the quality of his voice in *A Journey* and his interest in and openmindedness toward the Natives. Hearne is not innocent of remarks that today would be considered prejudicial and derogatory; however, he is overall passive, accepting, inquisitive, and curious as regards the Natives. This approach is distinct from the manner that other contemporary explorers wrote concerning Native populations. Hearne appears to take on the role of guest and observer. He hangs at the fringes and seems to understand that he is somewhat of a burden. He has moments of sympathy and deep feeling, and he possesses a love and empathy for his fellow creatures.

The character of Matonabbee I also built using Hearne's description contained within *A Journey*:

> Notwithstanding [Matonabbee's] aversion from religion, I have met with few Christians who possessed more good moral qualities, or few bad ones.
>
> It is impossible for any man to have been more punctual in the performance of a promise than he was; his scrupulous adherence to truth and honesty would have done honour to the most enlightened and devout Christian, while his benevolence and universal humanity to all the human race, according to his abilities and manner of life, could not be exceeded by the most illustrious personage now on record . . . (Hearne, 1795, p.224)

Matonabbee was indeed the most respected Chipewyan leader of his time, and he commanded a large following. Hearne does appear to ignore some troubling incidents. For example, Matonabbee beats one of his wives when the chief wants to fight for and add a woman to his already substantial number of women. The wife eventually dies from her injuries. Also, Matonabbee stabs the former husband of one of his wives because the wife pines for and wants to return to her former husband. The man survives the attack, and the wife eventually succeeds and leaves Matonabbee, who becomes depressed and disgruntled but does let her go.

Matonabbee did not, per reports, speak fluent English. He did most likely have a handle on most dialects of Athapaskan, various Cree dialects of Algonquian, as well as Western Siouan of the Assiniboine people. Sources hold that Matonabbee lived at the Fort from birth and was adopted by Richard Norton, Moses Norton's father, when his own Native father died (Glover, 1983). Richard Norton departed for England in 1741, and Matonabbee went to live with his Chipewyan relatives until he was sixteen. He was then hired at Prince of Wales Fort as a Home Guard, who were Native individuals that supplied the Fort with game, fish, firewood, and any other necessaries that were required for Fort maintenance.

My starting point for the character of Keelshies was an anecdote from Hearne's account. Hearne sees human bones on an island, which Matonabbee states are those of Copper Indians whom Keelshies lured toward Prince of Wales Fort under the pretense of accompanying his trading party. Keelshies and his party "stripped them of such parts of their clothing as they thought worthy their notice, went off with all the canoes, leaving them all behind on the island, where they perished for want" (Hearne, 1795, p.118).

Waawaatee is a fictional character, though Natives would have designated mostly men, less commonly women, as healers and spiritual leaders within their tribes. Though the Ojibwe were most famous for their sacred bundles, these were noted by employees and factors of the Bay and called "god bags" by the Europeans. HBC Factor Andrew Graham writes of "god bags":

> It is generally ornamented with paint, beads or brass-tags. It

contained medicines for his family, beaver teeth, bears-claws, eagles-talons, the beautiful red foreheads of woodpeckers, and may other kinds of feathers (Graham and Williams, 1767-1791), p.164).

The red leather chest that contained spices and ointments was gifted from the Forts to leaders of trading parties or their wives or a healer within the group (Ray & Freeman, 1978).

The story of Waawaatee's ancestor was a legend and myth of the Denesuline people. Hearne recounts the tale, which one presumes he heard during his extensive travels in their lands:

> There is a strange tradition among those people, that the first person who discovered those mines was a woman, and that she conducted them to the place for several years; but as she was the only woman in company, some of the men took such liberties with her as made her vow revenge on them; and she is said to have been a great conjurer. Accordingly when the men had loaded themselves with copper, and were going to return, she refused to accompany them, and said she would sit on the mine till she sunk into the ground, and that the copper should sink with her. The next year, when the men went for more copper, they found her sunk up to the waist, though still alive, and the quantity of copper much decreased; and on their repeating their visit the year following, she had quite disappeared, and all the principal part of the mine with her; so that after that period nothing remained on the surface but a few small pieces, and those were scattered at a considerable distance from each other. Before that period they say the copper lay on the surface in such large heaps, that the Indians had nothing to do but turn it over, and pick such pieces as would best suit the different uses for which they intended it (Hearne, 1795 pp.113–14).

Shenandoah Montour is a fictional character, though the Montours were a well-known, at times respected, at times infamous, family of translators that began with the marriage of Pierre Couc and Marie Miteouamegoukoué in Trois Rivere in the year 1657 (Hirsch, 2000). One of their daughters was Shenandoah's grandmother, known variously as Elizabeth, Isabelle and Madame Montour. She defected to the English with her brother Louis around 1706. Louis was murdered by the French in 1709 when leading groups of Natives from the Great Lakes Region to Albany. Madame Montour had a son Andrew who was active during the time of George Washington, and Washington did write the line about Andrew attributed to him in the novella. Andrew was a translator, emissary for the Native peoples, diplomat, and warrior who appears to have mostly sided with the English. He was noted for on and off sobriety, mostly off the latter part of his life. The description of his clothing comes from the Moravian missionary Count Zinzendorf (Lewin, 1966).

I would like to point out a few historical inaccuracies. First, the Chipewyans were, in all likelihood, not approaching Prince of Wales Fort by canoe in the year 1770. CG Davies writes that the Chipewyans "were hardly canoemen at all" (1965, p. XXIV). In the article "Changes in Territory and Technology of the Chipewyan," Beryl Gillespie writes,

> Chipewyan used canoes (and rafts) to cross rivers and lakes and to spear caribou at specific water crossings . . . Their canoes hold only one person. The rivers which water their country have no communication with Churchill River; for which reason it reduced them to the necessity of bringing their bundles on their backs (1976, p.9).

However, by 1790, Gillespie notes that the Chipewyans had learned to make canoes like the Cree and use them for waterway travel and the transport of furs to trading posts. Gillespie writes:

At Isle a la Crosse D. Thompson (1916:559) commented in 1791 on a small fleet of Chipewyan canoes. Between fifty and sixty small Canoes of Chepawyans were here . . . This present race have learned to build small Canoes of Birch Rind, and almost every way imitate their neighbours (1976, p.9).

I admit, I came upon this information after writing the scene that opens the book. The approach to Fort that I depict was common at other HBC Factories on Hudson's Bay and is described in detail by Factors Andrew Graham and James Isham. I chose to leave the approach as I felt it generally represented the ceremony and theater of the Natives' arrival, and in all honesty it was more exciting than my other openings. I also want to point out that a full watch at this time was four hours. In a few scenes, Jeremiah and Rodney appear to be on watch from before midnight until the morning.

Thank you for reading, and I hope to see you all again after I research and really start and finish my next book. I envision a narrative that spans from Montreal to Lake Athabasca, as Jeremiah continues to muddle and fuddle his way through life, his sister Agnes aspires to the echelons of Montreal society, and Waawaatee and Shenan rule a section of the Ottawa River, all with a backdrop of roguish and musical voyageurs. I look forward to continuing on this journey with you, the reader.

REFERENCES

Andra-Warner, E. (2003). *Hudson's Bay Company Adventures: The Rollicking Saga of Canada's Fur Traders*. Altitude Publishing Canada.

Bourrie, M. (2019). *Bush Runner: The Adventures of Pierre-Esprit Radisson* (First edition). Biblioasis.

Bown, S. R. (2020). *The Company: The Rise and Fall of the Hudson's Bay Empire*. Doubleday Canada.

Carlos, A. M., & Lewis, F. D. (2002). "Marketing in the Land of Hudson Bay: Indian Consumers and the Hudson's Bay Company." 1670–1770. *Enterprise & Society*, *3*(2), 285–317.

Carlos, A. M., & Lewis, F. D. (2001). "Trade, Consumption, and the Native Economy: Lessons from York Factory, Hudson Bay." *The Journal of Economic History*, *61*(4), 1037–1064.

Carlos, A. M., & Nicholas, S. (1990). "Agency Problems in Early Chartered Companies: The Case of the Hudson's Bay Company." *The Journal of Economic History*, *50*(4), 853–875.

Darrell, W. (1753). "The gentleman instructed, in the conduct of a virtuous and happy life. In three parts. Written for the instruction of a young nobleman. To which is added; a word to the ladies, by way of supplement to the first part." In *Eighteenth Century Collections Online* (13th ed.). Printed for Ignatius Kelly at the Stationers Arms in Mary's-Lane and John Exshaw at the Bible on Cork-hill.

Davies, K. G. (Kenneth G. (1965). *Letters from Hudson Bay, 1703–40*. Hudson's Bay Record Society.

Derbidge, G. "A History of the Drums and Fifes 1650–1700." *Journal of the Society for Army Historical Research*, vol. 44, no. 177, 1966, pp. 50–55.

Densmore, F. (1929). *Chippewa Customs*. United States Government printing office.

Ellis, H. (1982). *A Voyage to Hudson's-Bay by the "Dobbs Galley" and "California" in the Years 1746 and 1747 for Discovering a North West Passage : With an Accurate Survey of the Coast and a Short Natural History of the Country Together with a Fair View of the Facts and Arguments from which the Future Finding of Such a Passage Is Rendered Probable*. Printed for H. Whitridge.

Gillespie, B. C. (1976). "Changes in Territory and Technology of the Chipewyan." *Arctic Anthropology*, *13*(1), 6–11.

Glover, R. (1982). "Moses Norton (ca. Late 1720s–1773)." *Arctic*, *35*(3), 440–441.

Graham, A., & Williams, G. (1969). *Andrew Graham's Observations on Hudson's Bay, 1767–91*. Hudson's Bay Record Society.

Hearne, S. (1958). *A Journey from Prince of Wales's Fort in Hudson's Bay to the Northern Ocean, 1769, 1770, 1771, 1772*. Macmillan Company of Canada.

Hirsch, A. D. (2000). "The Celebrated Madame Montour: 'Interpretress' Across Early American Frontiers." *Explorations in Early American Culture*, *4*, 81–112.

Houston, C. S., Ball, T., & Houston, M. (2014). *Eighteenth-Century Naturalists of Hudson Bay*. McGill-Queen's University Press.

Isham, J. (1949). *Observations on Hudsons Bay, 1743, and Notes and Observations on a Book Entitled A Voyage to Hudsons Bay in the Dobbs Galley, 1749*. Published by the Champlain Society for the Hudson's Bay Record Society.

Knight, J. (2018). *Life and Death by the Frozen Sea : The York Fort Journals of Hudson's Bay Company Governor James Knight, 1714 1717* (A. J. Ray, Ed.). University of Toronto Press.

Laut, A. C. (1922). *The "Adventurers of England" on Hudson Bay : A Chronicle of the Fur Trade in the North*. Glasgow, Brook and Company.

Lewin, H. (1966). "A Frontier Diplomat: Andrew Montour." *Pennsylvania History*, *33*(2), 153–186.

Morice, A. G. (1906). "The Great Déné Race." *Anthropos*, *1*(2), 229–277.

Ray, A. J., & Freeman, D. B. (1978). *"Give Us Good Measure": An Economic Analysis of Relations Between the Indians and the Hudson's Bay Company Before 1763*. University of Toronto Press.

Rich, E. E. (Edwin E. (1958). *The History of the Hudson's Bay Company, 1670–1870*. Hudson's Bay Record Society.

Smith, J. G. E., & Burch, E. S. (1979). "Chipewyan and Inuit in the Central Canadian Subarctic, 1613–1977." *Arctic Anthropology*, *16*(2), 76–101.

Speck, G. (1963). *Samuel Hearne and the Northwest Passage*. Caxton Printers, Limited.

Stephen, S. P. (2019). *Masters and Servants: The Hudson's Bay Company and Its North American Workforce, 1668–1786* (first edition). University of Alberta Press.

Van Kirk, Sylvia. "Norton, Moses." *Dictionary of Canadian Biography*, vol. 4, University of Toronto/Université Laval, 2003.

Van Kirk, S. (1984). "The Role of Native Women in the Fur Trade Society of Western Canada, 1670–1830." *Frontiers (Boulder)*, *7*(3), 9–13.

www.ingramcontent.com/pod-product-compliance
Lightning Source LLC
LaVergne TN
LVHW041614070526
838199LV00052B/3134